Fros

CW01646260

Publication

Frost and Flame (A Cosy Christmas Romantic Fantasy Novella)

ISBN: 978-1-918118-10-0

Author Information

Why not join me on my social media accounts and keep up-to-date with what I'm currently working on:

On TikTok - @beccastormauthor

On Instagram – becca_storm_author

On Facebook: www.facebook.com/becca.storm.author.2025/

Explore more of my books at: beccastormbooks.co.uk

Frost and Flame

Written by Becca Storm

Chapters

Prologue

A Wistful Wish

The first snow of Christmas Eve had fallen thick and soft, blanketing the wee town in white. Children tumbled into the streets with shouts of laughter, their boots crunching through drifts, their mittens packed with snow. Snowmen rose like watchful sentinels, scarves tied askew, carrot noses crooked but proud.

Among them was Matthew, no more than eight, his cheeks pink from the cold. He crouched low behind a bank of snow, a perfect snowball cupped in his mitten. His friend's dark cap bobbed just beyond the drift, and with a grin, Matthew let his snowball fly. It struck true, bursting in a flurry of white.

Their laughter carried high into the crisp air, bright against the stillness of the winter woods beyond the town. The day was almost over, and the wonder and delight of what Christmas Eve would bring began to fill his joyful heart. But as Matthew caught his breath, his gaze shifted.

There, at the edge of the woods, a solitary figure moved across the snow. Mr Hale, tall, stooped, his coat collar turned high, carried an armful of logs toward his cottage. His footsteps were heavy, his expression unreadable, his form stark against the glow of lanterns and the merriment of the square.

The sight silenced Matthew's laughter. For a moment, he only watched, his small heart tightening with a feeling too big for words. Everyone knew Mr Hale lived alone. He did not join in the carols, or the market, or the Christmas Eve festivities. He was always apart, a shadow in the snow.

Matthew turned his eyes skyward. Stars pricked the darkening sky, faint and far away. Closing his eyes, he whispered, 'Please, let him find a friend this Christmas.'

The words vanished into the frosty air, carried upward like smoke from a chimney. And in the hush that followed, it grew as something stirred.

A glimmer of silver light shimmered across the treetops, a delicate frost unfurling over the branches like lace. Matthew gasped, eyes wide, as though the night itself had listened.

Somewhere in the woods, the promise of frost and a Christmas miracle awoke.

Chapter One

A Stranger in the Snow

Snow swirled down in lazy spirals, softening the edges of the quiet wee town. The streets were nearly empty, save for the glow of candles in the windows and the muffled laughter spilling from behind closed doors. Christmas Eve had always belonged to families, Daniel Hale thought as a shiver ran over his skin. Families and people who knew how to belong somewhere and how to cherish the love of their nearest and dearest. He didn't have that, and until tonight, it hadn't bothered him.

He tugged his scarf tighter and placed his hands in his coat pocket as he made his way along the cobbled street, boots crunching through fresh snow, a storm moving in along the hills on the other side of the town. The air was crisp, sharp and cold, his breath like smoke as it left his lips, rising to the thickening cloud above. There, strings of brightly coloured lights swayed in the wind, wrapped around branches, their glow catching and illuminating the drifting flakes as they gently floated down to a thick coating of snow.

He passed the bakery, shuttered and closed earlier than usual, so the owners could hurry home to enjoy their Christmas Eve celebrations. The bookshop, veiled in gloom, its windows dark and where a hand-painted sign wished all *A Merry Christmas.* It was strange to see these usually busy places, dark and lifeless, as they were generally brimming with happiness and joy.

His feet trudged on, the snow deeper as the heavier flakes swirled with more intensity. *A Winter Wonderland*, he thought as he took in the silent streets around him, admiring the gentle lights that paved his way. Christmas was far from his favourite time of year, but as he lifted his eyes and surveyed more of the quiet world around him, something stirred within him. He was so very tired of being on his own, living with only his own thoughts.

His house awaited at the edge of town, small and quiet and hidden in the dense trees on the edge of the woods. He could already picture the dark windows, the emptiness and the chill that lingered no matter how much he stoked the fire. He felt a reluctance to return there, to the gloom he had created. It was a lonely home and he had made it that way, but now, as he gazed at the wonder and beauty of the festive period brightening around him, he wished his home offered something more. The fresh notebook would await him, sat open on his desk inside, where it had waited for weeks—for words that never came.

Daniel sighed, stuffing his hands deeper into his coat pockets. This time of year was especially hard. The grief weighed down on his loneliness, and it took all he had to get out of bed. He had forced his feet into his boots and out onto the lane, hoping a little fresher air would release his writer's block. Words had always been a hard-earned expression of his inner self, and despite the enthusiastic readership he'd gained in the past, they'd never know how hard he battled to get those words onto the page.

He was so lost in thought that at first he didn't notice the light shimmer in the air. Frost bloomed across the windowpanes of the homes he passed as if painted by an invisible brush, curling into patterns of stars and vines. The air suddenly seemed to hum, bright but colder.

He stopped walking. His eyes fixed. Down the street, a figure moved—graceful, silent, almost gliding. She wore the palest blue, accompanied by a finely woven white woollen cloak, as though spun from snow. It had a hood adorned with thick white fur, masking the figure's face. The lamplight seemed to bend toward her, haloing her in silver. Her hand was outstretched, her fingers delicately stroking the air. Whenever her hand brushed a doorframe, frost blossomed and lingered, glittering in the radiance of her glow.

Daniel blinked hard, looking around to see if anyone else was witnessing this ethereal beauty, for he was sure he was imagining things, when fine coils of frost, delicate as lace, danced from her fingers. But then she turned, her face pale as moonlight, a glimmer of stardust gracing her eyes, sharp and luminous like the very stars themselves. And just for a moment, those eyes landed on him.

She froze.

As did he.

Chapter Two

By the Fire

The snow kept falling, soft as a feather, while the rest of the world held its breath. For a moment, time seemed to stop, and the world appeared to stand still as Daniel watched with anticipation and a lightness in his chest. She was the brightest and most unearthly being he had ever encountered, and he was utterly transfixed.

Then she spun as though to disappear, to melt back into the night like an imagined dream. He gasped as instinct tugged at him, and before he could stop himself, words left his lips as Daniel called out to her, his voice rough in the stillness as he moved his body toward her angelic like glow.

'Wait!'

She stilled again, her back to him, her fingers now lightly gripping the fur of her hood. Slowly, she turned as he approached her, and those starlit eyes fell on him again. Up close now, she didn't look entirely real. Her hair glimmered faintly, as though laced with ruins of frost, and the air around her glittered in fragments of frozen light. But her expression was wary and guarded, as though she expected him to recoil and flee.

'You can see me?' she asked in a bewildered whisper, her fine features drawn into a twisted confusion.

'I can see you,' Daniel said softly, more to himself than to her. 'You are real.' His voice was a mere murmur, his slate grey eyes wide with disbelief.

Her full violet lips parted, and the sound that escaped them was a whisper of winter air, like a precious Christmas carol to Daniel's lonely ears. 'You should not.' She stated firmly, yet light danced across her cold eyes.

Daniel stepped closer, hands lifted in submission, as if he might scare her. 'I don't mean any harm. I just…

You shouldn't be out here in the cold. The storm is moving closer; its snow will only deepen. Come inside and wait out the blizzard. My house is just down the lane.'

The words were unusual on Daniel's tongue. He never welcomed company and had grown so reclusive that he had not spoken to a single soul in weeks. To now be inviting this strange but charming vision into his home on Christmas Eve, shocked Daniel as much as it seemed to surprise her.

A strange smile flickered at her mouth. 'The cold does not trouble me.'

'Maybe not,' he admitted, 'but it troubles me, seeing you like this. A sacrifice to the storm.' He hesitated, heart hammering. 'Please.'

For a long moment, she only watched him, unreadable as the night sky. Her hair remained covered by that oversized fur hood, but he could see the tendrils of white that graced every strand. Then, with a slight incline of her head, she followed.

***

Daniel's cottage was dim when they entered, the only light coming from the glow of the fireplace, where embers pulsed a dull red. He busied himself at once, throwing on fresh logs until the flames leapt higher, casting golden light over the room that chased away the shadows.

Wringing his hands to relieve the cold and unsure of what to do now that she was here, he spun and stood behind his chair. ‘Here,’ he said, dragging the armchair closer to the hearth. ‘Sit and warm yourself.’

She moved with an ethereal grace, her presence filling the small room with a sense of wonder. The air crisped around her, the windowpanes slowly frosting over, a stark contrast to the warmth of the fire.

Daniel crouched by the hearth, stealing glances as he tended the flames. She looked at peace, utterly unaffected by this stranger's invitation. ‘I don’t even know your name.’

She tilted her head, eyes reflecting the firelight. ‘Names are for those who stay. I am only visiting... briefly.’

‘You’re not staying?’ A sadness filled his eyes. He didn’t much like company; it only magnified his grief, but she awakened something in him—a need to know her and understand who she was and where she came from.

There was a pause, a moment of hesitation. Then, almost reluctantly, she revealed a part of her mystery: 'Lumira. But you can call me Lumi.'

'Lumi,' he repeated, tasting it on his tongue. It suited her—cool, radiant, beautiful. Everything he felt he was not. 'I'm Daniel,' he said with quiet embarrassment. She was a vision in white, whilst he had struggled to drag his worn clothes over his body that morning.

Her gaze flicked from him to the notebook on his desk, its pages blank beneath the waiting pen. 'And what do you do, Daniel?'

The question struck him harder than it should have. He cleared his throat. 'I… write. Or I'm supposed to. Lately, it feels like I just stare at the paper. The words don't always come easy, but of late they seem to have failed me completely.'

Something softened in her eyes, like frost thawing under the first hint of spring. 'You should keep trying. Maybe you will find some inspiration in winter.'

He shrugged, his eyes revealing his doubt. 'I don't have much inspiration to put on the page. Winter so far has been bleak and uninspiring.' He revealed a lop-sided grimace.

She leaned forward, resting her chin on her hands, her eyes finding him. 'Then perhaps tonight you will find a story worth telling.'

Daniel's pulse jumped. He wanted to ask her a hundred questions—where she had come from, why the snow seemed to follow her. But more so, how she seemed to leave every surface she touched frost-bitten and faintly patterned like delicate lace. But none of those words made it past his lips. His words seemed to be failing him again. Instead, he drew his eyes to hers, and as her gaze rested on his, confidence found him as he quietly said, 'I think I have already found my story... my inspiration.'

She held his gaze, looking deep into his eyes, surveying him, as if weighing him up. As if she were trying to decide if he could be someone she could reveal her inner self to. The fire crackled, drawing her eyes as light began dancing with more vigour across the walls. The energy seemed to shift and change, a thrumming sensation around the room.

Inspiration suddenly sparked, and ideas rumbled around in Daniel's mind. He had not felt this need to write in so long. Outside, the snow continued to fall, growing heavier and more persistent as the world grew quieter and the words Daniel had been unable to find began to take shape.

He had an urge to put his pen to paper, to record this vision in white and the way in which winter seemed drawn to her, like she could control its frost and snow. He was drawn to her, too, and his mind was filled with words that needed to be spoken, words that needed to be shared.

Chapter Three

The Weight of Loneliness

The fire caught quickly, flames leaping and snapping in the grate. The large log engulfed in flames and heat as Daniel sat back on his heels, feeling the comforting warmth of the fire.

Lumi. That name instilled a deep yearning and warmth within him. A name meant to be recorded forever on the pages of a much-loved novel. Her beauty should be shared.

She sat perfectly still, as though carved from ice, yet the firelight danced across her like sunlight glimmering on early-morning snow. Her pale hair caught the light in silvery threads, and though her face was unearthly, her eyes seemed startlingly human—watchful, curious, touched with something like loneliness. An emotion he only knew and recognised too well.

He cleared his throat. 'Would you… Like something to drink? Tea? Cocoa? Maybe some mulled wine?'

Her lips curved faintly, a smile as thin as ice. 'If I touched it, it would freeze.' The contrast between the warmth of the fire and the coldness of her touch sent a shiver down Daniel's spine.

Daniel blinked. He wanted to argue, to insist she was wrong, but the words caught in his throat. Something told him she wasn't exaggerating. Instead, he gave a small laugh, half to cover his unease. 'Then I'll drink enough for both of us.'

He busied himself at the stove, filling the kettle, but stealing glances. She wasn't fidgeting or taking in the room like any ordinary guest might do. Instead, she sat, hands folded in her lap, eyes fixed on the fire like it was an unusual experience for her. The flames flared brighter where her gaze lingered, as though they, too, craved her attention and her touch.

When the kettle whistled, he poured himself a mug of hot cocoa and sat across from her, cradling the warmth. He let the sweet aroma tease his senses as the silence stretched for a moment longer, before finally asking, 'Why were you out there? It is terribly cold.'

Her head tilted, eyes finding his. 'It is my duty.'

'Your duty,' he repeated, unsure if he'd misheard.

'Yes.' Her gaze slipped back to the fire. 'On this night, every Christmas Eve, I walk the town. I bless the doors of the weary, the hearts of the lonely, and the minds of the hopeful. A touch of frost, a blessing given so good fortune follows.'

Daniel's brows knitted. 'You mean… the frost I saw on the windows?'

Lumi nodded once.

'That was you?'

Another nod.

He took a long sip of cocoa, partly for warmth, partly to buy him time. If she was mad, she was at least committed to the role. But something in him knew better. He'd seen her shimmer in the snow, seen the patterns bloom beneath her fingertips, and he'd felt something shift in the air when she'd looked at him.

'You don't expect me to believe that,' he said softly.

Her gaze snapped back to his, steady as a winter sky. 'And yet, you saw me. No one has seen me in many, many years.'

The fire popped. Daniel felt a chill run over his body, despite the heat.

'Why me? Why was I allowed to see you?' he asked with growing curiosity.

Her expression softened, a glimmer of something almost tender. 'Perhaps because you were looking.'

Startled, the words lodged in his chest. He swallowed hard, his throat suddenly too dry. For years, he had shut himself away, numbed by grief, his eyes always on the ground, as though by keeping them there, he could keep the world away. And yet tonight he had walked, eyes risen. Tonight, he had felt a need long forgotten. A desire to feel less alone. Tonight, he had looked up and he had seen her.

Daniel managed a fragile but genuine smile. 'Then maybe you're right. Maybe this is a story worth telling.' His demeanour had shifted, a spark of hope igniting in his eyes.

Lumi leaned back, folding her arms loosely, and for the first time, a sound like laughter escaped her—quiet, crystalline, like icicles chiming in the wind. It surprised him, yet warmed him to his core.

'You are a curious man, Daniel,' she murmured. 'Perhaps too curious.' The smile stretched as warmth blossomed on her cheeks.

'Maybe,' he admitted. 'But I'd like to know more. About you. About… all of this.' He smiled at her hopefully, a strange desire to know more sweeping through his chest.

Her eyes darkened, like steel and for a moment, he thought she might refuse. Then she said, 'The night is short. Ask, and I will answer—what little I can.'

Outside, the snow thickened against the windows—the winter wonderland and its quiet cold far away from the warmth growing inside the small cottage.

Where darkness once reigned, a light was growing. The moon hidden behind the clouds didn't stop the room from shining. Inside, the firelight flickered, wrapping them in a cocoon of warmth and shadow.

He stood then, moving to his desk as he gingerly picked up the pen and began making notes on the fresh, crisp page. His mind was filled with images and words that needed to be placed on the page, as if he was worried that if he didn't record them, they might slip away and be forgotten.

The pen moved with speed and grace across the page as Daniel furiously recorded every thought, every detail of this winter wonder before him. He was scared that if he missed any small aspect or feature, it would fade out of existence forever.

He felt her eyes on him as he kept his head low, focused on the pen and the words that were spilling across the many pages he had begun to fill with inspiration and need. She smiled as she watched, enthralled, as his eyes lifted softly and he set the pen aside.

'There,' he said. 'I have done what I have been fighting to do for many years. I have put pen to paper and released myself from the torture of writer's block.' He smiled as he beheld her, and she watched with fascination.

Rising, she made her way to the desk, standing by his side as her eyes rolled over his words.

'Inspiration has struck indeed,' she gasped, turning the page as the lingering lace of frost nipped at the page edges. She pulled her hands away, afraid her touch would spoil his words.

'Do you like what I have written? What I have begun to create?' He asked with trepidation, suddenly aware that her opinion mattered, maybe too much.

'It is the start of our story, and I like where it is going,' she confessed as her gaze met his.

They stood, their shoulders almost touching, as both their eyes fell upon the page. The night was yet young, and he had much more he wanted to say, to write, but he pulled himself from the page and decided then that he would live in the moment.

Chapter Four

A Night Out In Town

The fire had burned down to embers, and the clock on Daniel's mantel ticked steadily toward 9 pm. He should have felt tired, a creature of habit, he was always in bed by the time the sun left the sky. But something about Lumi's presence kept him wide awake. There was an energy in the room, a brightness that had been absent for so long and had nothing to do with the flames.

She sat in his chair still, watching the glow with a thoughtful expression, her hands folded loosely in her lap.

Frost shimmered faintly at her sleeves, a quiet reminder that she wasn't meant to be here. That time was ebbing away, that she shouldn't have been here at all.

Daniel set aside his empty mug and cleared his throat, his curiosity needing to know more. 'You've walked this town for… how long, did you say?'

'Centuries,' she replied.

'And when must you leave?' Daniel asked with trepidation, knowing she would at some point have to return to winter's call.

'I have until dawn,' she grimaced, her eyes filling with a sense of loss.

'And in all that time, walking these dark streets, you've never stopped to—' He hesitated, then gestured vaguely. 'To see it? The bakery, the square, the lights strung up every year?'

Her lips curved faintly, but it wasn't quite a smile. 'It is not my place to linger. My duty is to pass, unseen.'

'Well,' Daniel said, standing and offering her his hand, 'tonight, linger a wee while longer and see it with me.'

Her eyes flicked to his hand. Frost shimmered at her fingertips, and for a moment, he thought she might refuse. Then, almost shyly, she placed her hand in his.

Her touch was cold—startlingly so—but he didn't let go. Instead, he wrapped his fingers firmly around hers and the cold eased, softened, as if adjusting to him.

Together, Lumi, wrapped in her cloak of snow and fur, and Daniel, wearing his navy blue, long-length woollen coat, stepped out into the night. The snow had calmed, and only a few lazy flakes lingered as the stars began to penetrate the dark, night sky, and the moon reclaimed the darkness.

***

The town square lay hushed beneath a quilt of soft white snow, the golden lamplight glowing against the drifts that had settled across the town. Garlands drooped under the weight of frost, yet the shimmering lights within them released a soft glow. In the centre, the great pine tree stood tall, its branches heavy with snow and ornaments that glittered like tiny stars.

Lumi stopped, her starlit eyes wide. 'I have seen it only from a distance,' she whispered. 'It is beautiful.'

Daniel smiled. 'Come, then. Take a closer look.' He encouraged her, gripping her hand tighter and pulling her toward the square, her face alight with a childlike sense of awe.

They slowly approached the tree. Lumi's eyes trailed up its length as her gaze settled on the warm glow of the lights, encased between branches thick with pines. A glass ornament caught the light and reflected her face back at her—strange and luminous, framed in silver hair. She hadn't seen her reflection for such a long time. She reached out but didn't touch, her hand hovering just above the surface like she was afraid it might shatter.

'It is enchanting,' she said, voice hushed, eyes dancing with delight.

He found himself watching her instead of the tree, which was abundantly decorated with the spirit of Christmas. Reds and golds glimmered, red ribbons wrapped their soft lengths around the length in spirals, but it was her starlit eyes that held his attention. 'Yes,' he murmured, 'it is.'

They wandered slowly through the town square, past the bakery with its frosted windows and the café, where chairs were stacked for the holiday. Daniel pointed out little details—the crooked star someone had fastened on the lamppost, the toy shop's wooden reindeer with one antler missing. The stringed lights with one bulb dark.

Lumi laughed softly at that, a sound like icicles chiming, and Daniel felt his chest tighten at the music of her enjoyment. It warmed his ears and left the beginnings of a soft glow in his lonely heart.

'Why do you notice these things? These imperfections?' she asked him.

'Because they make the world feel real,' he said. 'Imperfect, but alive. It's the joy of finding the flaws in the beauty of it all that captures my attention.'

She was quiet for a long time, walking with him through the hush of snow, watching as the soft feathers of snow kicked up under her feet, leaving a perfect imprint of her dainty shoes. Then, almost too softly for him to hear, she said, 'I had forgotten how to see the world like that.'

He squeezed her hand gently, pulling his gaze to hers. 'Then maybe tonight is for remembering. Remembering a world of imperfection and beauty.'

Frost bloomed faintly along his hand where her fingers touched his, but it didn't nip or bite. Instead, it shimmered like starlight, like a swirl of tender warmth.

His heart beat faster at the sensation. She was beautiful, and he was having a hard time finding any imperfections in her.

For the first time in years, Daniel felt lighter. It took him by surprise as he realised it was not because the world had changed, but because he was seeing it—truly seeing it—through her eyes, as if he were witnessing the beauty of the world around him and all it had to offer for the very first time.

Memories long forgotten resurfaced, and as painful and unsettling as they were, he pushed deeper, where the glow in his heart grew stronger. He'd focus on that feeling, that warmth that was encasing his fragile heart, and perhaps, just maybe, she was now seeing the world through his eyes.

Chapter Five

A Frosted Pleasure

The square was alive with light when Daniel and Lumi wandered back through it. Strings of lanterns swayed above, casting soft halos on the snow, and music drifted from a gramophone someone had left playing near the market stalls. It made Daniel's heart soar to hear the wonder of Christmas all around him. At the far end, laughter rang out from the frozen pond that doubled as the town's ice rink. Lumi snapped her gaze to the laughter, intrigued.

She paused, her eyes wide. 'What are they doing?' Her expression was one of mystification at the enchanting call of those pleasant sounds of joy.

Daniel followed her gaze. The frozen pond had attracted couples who clutched each other's hands, sliding and stumbling across the gleaming surface. Girls spun like spinning tops, their scarves trailing behind them as their bodies became a spiral of blended colours. A young man fell, laughing, and a girl tugged him back to his feet before they darted away again, speeding off across the ice.

'Ice skating,' Daniel said. 'It's tradition. Every Christmas, the rink opens, and the whole town comes out.' His face lit up to an expression of wonder, his eyes shining as he observed the happy figures swirling and crashing across the ice.

Lumi tilted her head, transfixed. 'They play on the ice?'

'Something like that.' He glanced at her, smiling. Then a spark of inspiration tugged at him again. 'Would you like to try?' He asked.

She blinked, then laughed softly, crystalline as the frost around her. 'I walk on snow, Daniel. Ice will not trouble me.'

'It's not meant to trouble you. It is supposed to be fun!' He blinked as a falling snowflake caressed his eyelashes before melting and fading away. She looked at him, doubtful, but as his smile widened and mischief crossed his eyes, she allowed him to pull her toward the ice.

Minutes later, they stepped onto the frozen surface. Daniel's boots slipped immediately, and he flailed, catching her arm. She didn't waver. The frost beneath her feet seemed to welcome her, steadying her balance. She looked down at him, amused.

'You are clumsy,' she teased.

'And you're cheating,' he muttered, gripping her hand tighter, amusement dancing across his face.

She spun to face him, tugging him forward toward her. For a moment, he stumbled, but then the rhythm of her steps drew him into something like a dance. He was steady and smooth as he glided across the frozen pond, both his hands in hers. The world narrowed to the circle of their joined hands, the spin of snowflakes around them, and the music drifting through the cold air.

Daniel's laughter startled him—laughter that hadn't risen within him in years. It shook him to his core momentarily, but as he let the ripples of pleasure leave his body, he took solace in that strange feeling and allowed his mind to enjoy it.

'You're enjoying this,' Lumi said, her eyes sparkling. Her attention was drawn only to Daniel and the light that seemed to be finding his eyes.

'Only because you haven't let me fall…yet!' He chuckled as he swept around her, with more confidence and grace, allowing his feet to spin and spiral.

Her lips curved. 'I would never let you fall.'

The words hung between them, heavy with more than play. Daniel's chest ached as he met her gaze, but before he could speak, children skated past with shouts of joy, breaking the spell.

'Hey, Mr Hale. It's nice to see you. Do you wish to join us?' The smaller child said with hope. His eyes seemed to burn into Daniel in a way that showed pity, as though he felt sorry for him.

Daniel smiled, 'I'm fine here, Matthew, with my companion,' he responded with warmth.

'Oh, all right. I didn't want you thinking you had to be out here on your own.' Matthew's smile faded as the hope of relieving Daniel's loneliness weighed down on him. He skated off, glancing back over his shoulder, his eyes filled with a lingering sadness.

'He can't see you?' Daniel gasped as he questioned Lumi, realising he must have appeared a little mad, squeezing the air with his hand and chatting to himself.

Lumi nodded. 'No one can. Only you have been given the ability to see me,' she smiled warily, worried this might push Daniel away.

'Perfect! I have you all to myself,' he grinned sheepishly, but the light that was donning his eyes grew more intense for a lingering moment.

They took another few turns around the frozen pond, their laughter escaping into the night air, but all the time, Daniel was aware that others watched him. They seemed pleased to see him looking so happy, less reclusive, but their eyes were wary all the same.

When at last they left the rink, Daniel's cheeks hurt from smiling, his hands numb from the cold. Lumi looked luminous, her cloak shimmering with a dusting of frost, her hair catching the lamplight like spun silver.

'Come on,' he said, leading her out of the square and past the large pine tree. 'After skating, there's only one thing to do.'

Lumi looked at him with curiosity, wondering what he meant, but Daniel only gripped her hand tighter and pulled her down the path. His body was filled with excitement, like he was about to reveal the world's longest-kept secret. She smiled and followed, keen to learn more.

By the time they returned to Daniel's cottage, the snow had fallen again with vigour and was piled high against the door. He pushed it open with his shoulder, laughing as flakes tumbled in after them, covering the floor with a layer like ice.

Lumi slipped inside like a shadow, her frost trailing across the threshold, as he shut the door firmly behind them, blocking the colder tendril of deep winter from entering. The room felt warmer than before—not because of the fire, but because of the way she lingered close by, her silver gaze fixed on him as though she couldn't quite look away. It felt like she was just as mesmerised by him as he was by her.

He shook the snow from his coat, hanging it on the hook by the door and gestured toward the hearth. 'Sit. I'll stir up the fire again.'

Obediently, she lowered herself into the chair. The flames caught quickly, leaping high into the air. For a moment, Daniel watched her in the glow, his chest tight with something he couldn't name. His frosted edges melting as he took her beautiful face in.

He moved eagerly to the kitchen, rummaging in his icebox, and triumphantly produced a large, square tub covered in frost.

Following him to investigate the noise, she looked at him with curiosity. 'What is that?' Lumi asked as she watched, bemused, as he spooned its frozen contents into two bowls.

Wiggling his eyebrows, he chimed, 'Something you can't freeze but will almost certainly enjoy!'

Stepping forward, Lumi gazed at the strange, frozen mixture inside the tub. Gasping, she stilled. 'You eat… frozen milk?' she asked.

Daniel grinned. 'Trust me.' He took a bite, closing his eyes with exaggerated delight. 'Christmas isn't Christmas without ice cream. He took a lump of the white ice cream, smoothing it onto Lumi's spoon, and handed it to her. 'Try it!'

Lumi lifted her spoon to her mouth and slowly opened her lips. The cold metal with the frozen mixture met her tongue. She didn't flinch as the cold didn't bother her, but the taste… that surprised her.

For a heartbeat, her expression was unreadable—then her eyes widened, and the faintest flush of rose bloomed across her pale cheeks. She looked from her empty spoon to the bowl, taking another spoonful and quickly popping it in her mouth.

'It melts,' she whispered. 'It is cold, but it melts with sweetness. A taste I have longed for, for so long.'

'Exactly.' Daniel watched her, heart twisting. 'Cold, but sweet. Just like you.' He grinned as a flush crossed his cheeks.

Her laughter spilt into the room, soft and bright. They took their bowls and ate together by the fire, snow tapping gently at the windows, and for the first time, Daniel felt as though Christmas might finally belong to him again.

Chapter Six

A Past Long Forgotten

That winter had been the cruellest. Snow had fallen for weeks without end. The skies had remained dark, and no light shone, hinting at an end to the ongoing suffering. The undulating cold penetrated every surface, both outside and within.

Lumi remembered it in fragments—the muffled hush of a world buried deep under snow, the way smoke rose thin and weak from chimneys where no wood remained left to burn. The homes had as much frost collecting on the inside of the windows as they did on the outside. And then there were the gaunt faces of neighbours whose eyes had grown too large for their hollow cheeks.

Some eyes bore the sign of a gut-wrenching grief. Children had fallen into an eternal slumber while trying to warm their thin bodies and frozen feet. The animals had been the first to whither, and the thin carcasses of their bodies had kept the townsfolk fed for a while, but that supply of food was now gone. The cupboards and pantries were bare. The crops had failed, and the larders were empty. That winter of Lumi's youth had not been a gentle one. It came early, with a hunger sharper than wolves.

Her village had been small, nestled at the edge of the forest. They had always endured lean months, but that year the fields had frozen before the harvest could be brought in. Wheat stood stiff and ruined beneath ice. The root cellars emptied too quickly. By the second month, people spoke less of feasts and more of basic survival.

Lumi's father broke their last chair for firewood. Her mother wept as the flame devoured it, because it meant no seat for the baby that had already withered in her arms.

Night after night, the villagers gathered in the chapel, their breath misting in the freezing air, as they prayed for a thaw. They begged for mercy. They cried for the lost souls taken too young. They wished for a spring warm and freeing, but the sky remained steel, the frost unrelenting. Their misery lingered on.

Lumi had been little more than a girl on the verge of adulthood, but she remembered the sharp ache of hunger twisting her belly, the way her lips split from the cold. The muscles in her body, once firm, were shrunken and withered like the wheat stalks beneath the frost. The silence where laughter should have been was replaced with misery and despair. Grief-stricken moans and silent tears replaced what had always been a happy town. She remembered the children dying first, then the elderly succumbed to the bleak darkness not long after.

And she remembered the moment hope snapped.

It was her mother's eyes—dull, unfocused, no longer pleading. She had given up and lost all hope. The village had nothing left to give, no voice strong enough to carry a prayer. That was when Lumi stole away into the forest, barefoot in the snow, her heart a raw wound of desperation. Her body stumbled as the energy needed to navigate the deep, snow-covered paths had slowly ebbed away, with the months passing and little food.

But she pushed on. Her mother's emptiness spurring her to keep going. The moon lit the clearing, pale and merciless. Her knees struck the ground first, and her body collapsed, the energy gone and her feet frozen, toes blackened with frost. She cried out, voice breaking as the will to live on depleted, into the silence of the endless winter.

'Take me. Take whatever I have, only spare them. Let them live, and I will bear the cold. I will walk it, serve it, forever.' Lumi fell forward, her hands now deep in the snow, her head hanging, and her body aching. Her muscles trembled as the frost sank deep within her, chilling even her bones.

The night stirred. Frost blossomed across the ground in delicate, curling patterns, racing toward her in a brilliant blue like an answer. The trees glittered with sudden ice, like glass; it was sharp and hostile. And the air thickened—not with warmth, but with a presence.

The frost had heard her.

When she stood again, her tears had frozen on her cheeks; her hair was streaked with silver, though she was barely a young woman. Her skin no longer burned with cold as a stillness encased her. Suddenly, she was shielded in a cloak of white with a brush of fur around the hood.

She walked back to the village with a gift in her hands—frost that would spare their food, ice that would preserve what little they had, snow that could be turned to water. She brought the promise of wood to burn and heat to melt the frost encasing every home.

And so her people lived. The winter receded, and the sun began to light up the steel sky; the long-awaited crops returned the following spring. Children laughed as they played again in the thaw. Their fingers and toes were warmer with the heat of the rising sun.

But Lumi never thawed. She remained trapped in winter as frost claimed her fingers.

Year after year, she returned only as frost's shadow, watching her family thrive in their abundance of food and wood to burn, yet their expressions were grim. Lumi was lost to her people forever, and as time passed, her name faded on the lips of those she saved. Until at last, no one remembered her at all.

Chapter Seven

Secrets and Stories

Watching her with quiet regard, Daniel finally broke the silence. 'You've been walking this town for centuries,' he said finally. 'Why? What keeps you tied to it but not part of it?'

Lumi was silent for so long he wondered if she would answer. Her fingers traced idle patterns on the armrest, frost blooming into patterns of lace, beautiful and perfect, before fading beneath her touch.

'When I was young,' she began at last, her voice quiet, 'my people were starving. Winter came early, and the crops failed. The cold did not lift for months. Children died in their mothers' arms. Families burned their last scraps of wood.'

Daniel's breath caught. 'And you? Your family?'

'My family suffered too. Everyone suffered. No one escaped its cold tendrils. It was the cruellest winter. With nothing left to give, I prayed for deliverance,' she said, memories staining on her serene face, her eyes darkening as she recalled a painful past, 'And the frost… it answered.'

Her gaze lifted, distant, as though she were looking back through centuries to memories so detached from who she was now that recalling them must have been difficult and painful. 'It offered me a bargain. To walk the earth in winter's name. As spirit of the frost, I could offer blessings to the living. I could heal their grief, fill their hungry tummies, and bestow them with fortune and plenty. Never again would they suffer at the cruel hands of winter.'

She paused. Her eyes were colder, like she was reliving the choice she made. A choice that would ensure her people would never starve or go hungry again—a choice she had made to save them.

'In return … if I surrendered my own life, my mortal existence to the Goddess of Winter, my people would never suffer. They'd never again have to endure a winter like the one they were facing. So, of course, I said yes.' She stilled as her eyes darkened and looked like they could almost shed a tear.

'The unnecessary death of babes so young, it seemed like the only choice I had left to make.' She drew her eyes back to the flaring flames, which danced and coursed with newfound fury, as though reacting to the bargain made.

'I thought it would be just one winter. Perhaps two. But I was wrong.' She swallowed then, her throat pressing hard against her smooth, pale skin.

Eyes softening, her hands again folded in her lap, she appeared frozen, like ice. 'I learned, as others did, bargains do not end when mortals wish them to. We surrendered to the winter, and our fate was in her hands.'

Daniel's chest ached. 'So, you gave up everything?' He questioned, his eyes filling with understanding, as admiration rose for her sacrifice and choice.

'I gave up belonging. I gave up warmth. I gave up a home and a family to ensure others did not suffer the same.' Her eyes met his, luminous in the firelight as the silence breathed around the room. Daniel shifted in his chair, heart heavy with her truth. Her past was just as painful as his had been, if not more.

'I became a shadow of frost, a spirit of winter, and I returned each year to do as I was bound. I saved my village. I released the yearly pain that winter often brought. But I didn't know the bargain's true cost.' She shivered then as though she was finally feeling the cold again. But Daniel knew it wasn't the frost that spurred that shiver. It was the past and its many memories.

'No one could speak to me. No one could see me. No one mortal anyway. I've lived in solitude since then, yearning to return to my family. Well, that was until tonight.'

The weight of her loneliness struck him harder than any of her otherworldly revelations. Centuries, walking unseen, unnoticed, unheard. His own grief, sharp as it was, suddenly seemed so small beside hers.

Daniel reached across the space between them, covering her cold hand with his warmth. For an instant, frost crackled across his skin, glittering like tiny stars. But he didn't let go. He'd been allowed this one special night to see her, and he wouldn't break that bond.

'You're not alone tonight,' he said quietly. His words rang like truth to his ears. He realised then that she was not the only one lingering on the outside, never being seen. He, too, held that hope in his heart that one day, he'd be brought back into the warmth, again be truly seen.

He hadn't chosen the path life had taken him down, and despite turning from the world and living in the shadows, he felt he had deserved more. More than what the world had given him and so cruelly taken away.

Something flickered across her face—fragile, almost fearful, but undeniably hopeful. Her lips parted as if to speak, then closed again. She only nodded.

They sat in silence for a long time, the fire painting the room gold while the storm again pressed against the windows. And though nothing more was said, Daniel knew the truth: a single night with her already meant more to him than the years he'd been without her.

Chapter Eight

Winter of Despair

The memory came to him not with warning, but with the hush of snowfall against the window. Perhaps it was the way the firelight flickered across Lumi's face, or the way her eyes seemed to search the shadows in him. Either way, Daniel found himself pulled backwards into the winter he had tried so hard to bury.

He had once lived in a house not unlike this one—warm, bustling, full of sound and buried in the heart of their wee town. His wife, Clara, had been a flame in every sense: laughter that filled a room, hands always busy with kindness, eyes that caught his whenever words failed him. The house had always smelled of cinnamon and fresh bread, and the neighbours visited daily, keen to spend time with the woman who offered so much.

She was an ear for the troubled, a warm embrace for the weary, and a beacon of hope for the wounded, and she enchanted everyone she met with her quiet regard and enormous heart. She was also the most fulfilled at Christmas and insisted that Christmas wasn't a day but a season to be lived in. It was a time to spend with family and those who were dear, and everyone she knew was to live that magic with her.

They had dreamed of a family — Daniel and Clara — and a house in the city with a white picket fence and flowers blooming brightly in every bed around the manicured lawn. A garden with trees large enough to live in, that should be climbed with a tree house that was a haven and a place to keep their children's memories and secrets. And for a while, that dream had seemed possible. It was tangible and just within reach. An exciting future filled with possibilities and a life full to the brim with love and belonging.

But the winters grew long, and the hope of children began to fade. Clara's health began to falter, and she seemed to lose a small part of her charm and loving nature with every passing day. By the time the doctors were called to see her, they spoke the words 'too late,' and Daniel's heart had already known. He had watched the light fade from her day by day, and though he begged for more time, more miracles, there was no frost to bargain with, no spirit to answer his prayer. He felt utterly alone in it all as he felt his heart fade with hers.

One December night, as the snow fell vigorously and the moon dipped behind the clouds of the approaching storm, she closed her eyes and slipped from him quietly, as though she didn't want to disturb his grief with her passing. The house that had always been too small for their joy suddenly became cavernous in its silence. It darkened as her missing presence veiled that house in misery and a grief he could never escape.

After those torturous, grief-filled months when spring began to bloom, Daniel had tried to live again. As much as his heart was not in it, he had moved to the cottage where he now resided and turned his attention to his writing. However, the world had grown crueller, even more brutal. As he tried to lose himself in his work, the words failed him. He couldn't find anything to put on the page, as his thoughts and ideas were locked away deep inside. As the frustration grew and the grief continued, he stopped writing. He just looked at the blank page and felt nothing stir within him.

Words had once been his gift, but now every page mocked him as they remained white and untouched. Every story felt false, and his mind couldn't release the words to tell it. The truth was that the one story he wanted to write—the one he so badly wanted to tell- had died along with Clara. It could only be written with Clara alive and by his side. But that wasn't possible, for she was gone and so were his words, his passion and his muse.

He withdrew, locking himself in his own quiet misery. He lingered in solitude and silence. Invitations to dinners went unanswered, and carols went unsung. Neighbours who had felt his grief so vividly were always turned away and finally stopped knocking. His cottage at the edge of town became less a home than a hollow, where he sat by the fire with nothing but the ache of memory and words he could not say. He was isolated, alone and locked in his own mind.

The world moved on. Children grew, couples married, and lights filled the town each Christmas. But Daniel carried winter inside him, colder than any snow outside. He told himself he deserved it—because he had failed to save her, because he had no words left to speak life into anything and his light had been taken away.

And that is how it had been for many years… Until tonight. Until the frost blessed his door, and the frost-eyed woman with the stars in her eyes, who had dared step inside, reminded him that even in winter, even in the grief of painful memories, miracles might still find him and his lonely heart.

Chapter Nine

The Spark of Longing

The storm outside had quieted, snowflakes drifting more slowly past the windows. The fire burned steadily now, filling the room with a soft glow. Daniel leaned back in his chair, his hand still resting lightly over Lumi's. He felt at peace for the first time in so long. His body radiated contentment, and he was glad of it.

He half-expected her to pull away, but she didn't. Her gaze remained on the flames, though he could see the delicate tremor of her breath, the way her fingers curled slightly as if she wanted to hold on. *Was she feeling like he was? Was she feeling the peace as he was?*

It was a comfortable silence, but to break the stillness, Daniel rose and crossed to the corner to where his old piano sat. It hadn't been touched in months—maybe years but he had a sudden urge to feel the cool keys beneath his fingertips. Dust clung to the top, but when he lifted the lid and positioned his fingers, he pressed a key, and the note rang out, warm and low.

Lumi tilted her head. 'What is that?'

He looked back at her, startled. 'You don't know?'

Her lips curved faintly. 'I have watched villages rise and fall, Daniel. But music, I have only heard from a distance.'

Daniel swallowed and sat down on the bench. He straightened his shoulders and again positioned his hands. 'Then tonight, you'll hear it up close.'

His fingers fumbled over the keys for a few moments, and then they found a simple melody. He was hesitant at first, but soon smoothed into something gentle, like snow drifting from the sky. Deep notes spilt out lazily and filled the room, weaving around the crackle of the fire, tender and unhurried. Daniel sighed. He had forgotten how much joy this had once given him. The beauty of the music, a captivating force, drew in all who heard it.

Lumi slowly rose from her chair, drawn forward as though the sound itself beckoned her. She stood by Daniel's side at the piano, her eyes wide, her face unguarded in wonder.

'It is…' She struggled for the word. '…alive.'

Daniel smiled faintly. 'That's how it feels when I play, although I haven't played for some time.'

For a long moment, neither moved as the notes echoed faintly in the air around them, Lumi's ears keen to hear more. Then he shifted, leaving space on the bench, signalling with a soft pat of his hand to the seat beside him. Hesitant, almost shy, she moved around him and made her way toward the space, lowering herself onto the bench. Her shoulder brushed his, cool against his warm skin, and he felt his pulse quicken.

He played softer now, aware of every breath she took, every slight tilt of her head as she listened. When the final note faded, silence fell again—but it was a different silence. It was charged, expectant.

Lumi turned to him. Her eyes glimmered like ice catching firelight, fragile and fierce all at once.

'That was wonderful. I have never enjoyed music more. But why do you show me these things?' she whispered.

He smiled then and caught her hand in his, the keys dipping as he did, and a soft note invaded the air. Lumi laughed lightly as though she were a child exploring a new toy and had been caught off guard by an unexpected sound.

Daniel squeezed her fingers. 'Because you deserve to see these things,' he said. 'Because you deserve more than loneliness.'

Her lips parted, trembling faintly. 'But what if I cannot have more? At dawn, the Goddess will come to claim me. She will take me from you.'

He swallowed hard then, his eyes finding hers. 'Then I'll be grateful for every moment until she does.'

The words seemed to hang between them, warm enough to thaw the air. Slowly, as if drawn by something greater than either of them, Daniel leaned closer, her cold breath frosting his lips. He paused, giving her the choice.

Lumi's breath caught—but she didn't pull away. Instead, she leaned forward, and as her eyes flashed with warmth, she closed the distance.

Their lips met, cool and warm at once, and the kiss was soft and tender, hesitant yet filled with the aching sweetness of something that felt both fragile and inevitable. Frost bloomed and spread across the piano keys beneath her hand, shimmering in silver of the most delicate lace.

His hand moved to her waist as he pulled her closer, deepening the embrace, and Lumi didn't hesitate, returning his need with her own. Her hand found his cheek, as she held his face in her palm, and the spirals of frost tenderly danced across his skin. His spine tingled and his heart soared. He hadn't felt this alive in years.

The kiss lingered for a few more moments, then they slowly drew back. Lumi's eyes shone with something unspoken—longing, fear, and a sense of wonder. She smiled and closed her eyes as though savouring the moment —the feel of his lips on hers.

Then the moment was broken as the clock on the mantel chimed midnight. The sound echoed like a reminder, sharp against the softness of their embrace. Time was ebbing away, and it was a truth Daniel couldn't escape from. Time was running out, and soon she would be gone.

Lumi closed her eyes, shaking her head slightly, her words almost failing her. ‘The night grows short,’ she whispered. ‘And so does my time.’

Daniel sighed and brushed a hand gently along her cheek, his heart aching. ‘Then let’s not waste it.’

Chapter Ten

A Gift of Healing

Laughter filled the air as the night pressed on. The kitchen was a mess, and the cottage had never felt warmer.

Flour dusted the counters, sugar sparkled like frost across the kitchen table, and somewhere near the stove, a spoon had gone missing entirely. Daniel stood in the centre of it, his apron streaked with chocolate, laughing so hard his ribs ached.

'I told you,' he said, pointing at the lumpy, half-collapsed yule log. 'You can't just *stare* at the sponge and expect it to rise.'

Lumi, perched lightly by the kitchen window, tilted her head in mock dignity. 'It was worth a try.' A dusting of flour clung to her silver hair like snow, her fingers splattered with the lumpy mixture, but she didn't even seem to notice.

Despite her protests, she had joined him in every step—measuring, stirring, even rolling dough—though she could not linger near the oven. Whenever her hand brushed a warm tray, frost crept along the metal until Daniel shooed her back with laughter.

Still, she had found her own delights. She shaped star cookies with delicate precision, carving tiny patterns into the dough with a fingertip of frost. Daniel had never seen anything so beautiful or so impractical, yet half of them had cracked in the heat. Lumi had only smiled, as though imperfection was part of the charm. 'Perfect, but alive. Flawed yet beautiful,' she said as she repeated Daniel's earlier words.

By the time the mince pies were cooling on the sill, the room glowed with the warmth of oven heat and something gentler, more elusive. Daniel leaned against the counter, breathless, watching Lumi dust sugar across the ruined yule log with the solemnity of a queen bestowing a crown.

‘It looks dreadful,’ he said. ‘I don’t think even your splendid arrangement of sugar will save it!’

She glanced at him, eyes alight. ‘It looks like joy.’ Her eyes fell again to the yule log, and she beheld it as if it were the best creation to have ever been made.

And somehow, he could not argue.

***

Later, when the chaos had been cleared away and the kitchen restored to something resembling order, Daniel poured two mugs of mulled wine. Lumi cradled hers carefully, leaning against the counter, though the steam made her fingers tremble.

‘Thank you,’ she said softly. ‘For tonight. For all of it. I had forgotten how laughter feels when it fills a room.’

Daniel smiled, his heart aching with warmth. ‘Then we’ll keep laughing, together, you and I.’

Her gaze lingered on him, unreadable. Then, slowly, she lifted her hand. Frost spiralled from her fingertips, not wild and curling as before, but deliberate, delicate. It spilt across the worktop, slow and precise as crystals bloomed in a graceful pattern—stars and snowflakes woven into a lattice of silver light. At the centre of the worktop, the frost shaped itself into the image of a pen and piano, careful and shimmering.

He stared, throat tight. Eyes tracing the fine and delicate formation of those images, and his heart beat a little faster. The stars and snowflakes fluttered around her creation and melted his heart.

'It is all I have to give, but these moments filled me with such joy,' Lumi whispered. 'A gift that will melt, like me. But it is yours to remember, like I always will.'

Daniel reached out, brushing his fingers lightly across the drawings. He admired the shapes surrounding the pen and piano, as if they were the finest piece of art he had ever laid eyes on. Cold stung his skin, but he didn't care. 'It's perfect," he said hoarsely. "Because it's from you."

She smiled then—a fragile, luminous thing—and for a moment the whole world seemed to glitter like frost beneath dawn.

They stared at each other, no further words needed to be spoken. This night had meant the world to them both, as each, lost in their own silence and misery, had somehow been released from that loneliness by a strange twist of fate.

He had seen her when he shouldn't have, and this allowed her to see him, too. His grief had almost broken him, and tonight she was witnessing the true fibres of his being, seeing the man beneath the shadows and the light within his heart.

As they sipped on their mulled wine, the now tepid warmth filled Lumi's chest, and she realised that for the first time in centuries, she felt like she belonged. She felt as if she had been seen and heard, and it had not escaped her that, when the dawn came and the Goddess drew her back, her heart might shatter like frozen glass.

Chapter Eleven

A Bond of Warmth

The cottage was quiet but for the crackling and popping of the fire as it devoured another log. The storm outside had hushed and softened, leaving only a forgiving patter against the windows and the steady rhythm of Daniel's breath.

He and Lumi sat close, closer than they had ever dared before. Now, on the sofa as opposed to the armchairs they had earlier been sitting in, his arm was wrapped around her shoulders, resting across the white fur of her hood, as her hand rested within his. It was a fragile and cool touch, the frost of her fingertips making his skin prickle even through the reignited heat from the hearth. He knew he should have pulled away. He was leading his heart to an inevitable ache when the dawn rose, but instead, he held tighter.

Her eyes met his, silver glimmering brightly within her starlit gaze that he had not seen in them before. It spoke of hunger, fierce and aching, not for food or for warmth, but for him—a need to have him as hers.

'Daniel,' she whispered, her voice catching him by surprise as the sound of his name on her lips was almost enough to undo him. It spoke to his heart, not just his ears.

He leaned forward then, as their mouths met, and this kiss was nothing like the soft, tentative embrace they had shared before. This one was more urgent, all-consuming, a collision of cold and warmth that stole the breath from both their lungs. It was unexpected and driven by utter need and lust—a moment filled with a desire to come together and touch each other's skin.

Her fingers slid into his hair, sending rivulets of frost trailing down the nape of his neck. His hands gripped her waist, feeling her tremble beneath his touch. They pressed together, drawn by only a need to touch each other. This kiss was deeper than the last, until words were impossible to express and only an unravelling want remained.

Daniel pulled Lumi to her feet as his fingers found the edge of her cloak, and running his fingertips along the smooth, soft fabric, he tugged it aside. She gasped, her body arching into his, as he undid the tie at her neck, and the cloak fell to the floor, a puddle at their feet.

His eyes traced the lower cut lace edging of her light blue silk dress, which caught the warmth lingering in the air. She felt desperate and afraid all at once. He pulled her closer, her chest firm against his as her chill began searing against his heat.

Their lips found each other again, deep and hungry, as their arms wrapped around the other, their fingers exploring the contours of each other's shapes. He began walking her backwards, toward the room just off the hallway at the entrance to the cottage. She was oblivious as he continued to kiss her, his fingers roving over her slender waist, her hands again in his hair and gripping the nape of his neck.

The door swung open with a thud as it hit the dresser, and he swept her up in his arms and placed her gently on the bed. She looked up at him with desire, her head reclining on his soft white pillow as he gently lowered himself down on the bed beside her. He watched her intensely as he placed a hand on her tummy, his fingers stroking the smooth silk of her dress, and they roamed higher.

She again arched her back as his fingertips gently rippled across her breasts, finding the lace embellishments at the edge of her low-cut neckline, and a groan left his throat, deep and warm.

Her fingers found his shoulders as she pulled him closer to her, and he leaned over her trembling body as their kiss again deepened.

'Stay,' he murmured between kisses, his lips grazing her jaw, her throat, soft but firm. 'Stay with me. Don't go.'

Her fingers clutched his woollen jumper, running along the V-neck collar that pressed against his skin. Beneath her touch, she could feel the soft spirals of his chest hair, the taut muscles across his shoulders and her breath shuddered. She took a steadying lungful of air. 'I want to stay. You have no idea how much being with you would mean to me.' She closed her eyes, her lips gently caressing his again.

'Then stay. Lie with me and let the sun rise. Just stay here… with me!' He whispered between kisses, his lips cooling against her lips.

'If I do… I could unmake you. Your fire would falter. And my frost… would break apart in your warmth.' She said, suddenly turning serious as her glittering eyes found his again.

He pulled back slightly, his hands stilled, the weight of her words sinking into him. *Would their joining of desire and need really tear them apart?* He knew she was right—their very natures pulled in opposite directions. They were polar opposites in every aspect. To lie together as he longed to might mean the end of them both.

And yet neither of them let go. They held each other, eyes staring intensely into the other's, and they just held on, for the want and need of it, despite the dangers.

He pressed his forehead to hers, their lips brushing in a trembling half-kiss. Her breath came in clouds against his cheek. 'We cannot,' she whispered.

'I know,' Daniel said, voice raw. 'But it doesn't stop me from wanting to.' His eyes shut as though he were saying a silent prayer.

Her fingers tightened in his hair, her whole body pressed to his as if she might brand herself into his memory. 'I want this, too.'

For a long time, they held each other—kissing, touching, drawing back before the fire and frost could destroy one another, yet never loosening their grip. Their embrace was a fragile defiance, a promise unfulfilled but burning all the same.

At last, she buried her face against his chest, her voice muffled and aching. 'The night is short. But while it lasts, I am yours.'

Daniel closed his eyes again, arms wrapped fiercely around her. 'And I am yours.'

They stayed like that, fire and frost bound in a fragile harmony, lying close enough to feel the burn of frost or heat, yet knowing it might destroy them. Going any further was a risk, and if they allowed the layers of clothing to slip from between them, this intense, fragile union may be the end of them. Yet, the night would not last forever, and it was a gnawing pain that filled both their chests.

But something within them had shifted. No matter how briefly, their loneliness had lifted, and for one short night, they had been allowed to be close to another being, to share experiences and secrets that had never passed their lips until that night. It was brief and exciting, but the reality of what they faced come dawn was a lingering thought as the clock ticked steadily and the sun promised to rise again in the dark, winter sky.

Chapter Twelve

A Little Christmas Light

The scent of cinnamon and sugar still lingered in the kitchen when Daniel tugged open the tall, thin cupboard in the corner of the room. Boxes clattered as he dragged them out, spilling their contents across the kitchen floor—tangles of garland, a battered angel with a crooked halo, wooden ornaments carved long ago.

Lumi tilted her head, watching curiously as she reclined on the armchair, again back by the hearth, as her eyes found the chaos Daniel was creating. Looking through the archway that led to the kitchen, she asked, 'What is all this?'

Daniel grinned, brushing dust from his hands. 'Tradition. If you're going to bake mince pies on Christmas Eve, you've got to have the tree too. It is always at the heart of Christmas.'

She heard the back door open, and the cold air raced in as she made her way to the arch, her fingers delicately grazing the beams as frost travelled in slow, lingering spirals across the dark surface. Her gaze shifted to the tall fir tree now standing in the centre of the chaos, its branches dusted with the snow that had clung when he'd dragged it to the back door that morning. It stood bare now, noble but stark.

'It is a perfectly handsome tree.' She said with sincere honesty. 'What are you planning to do with it?' She questioned, her eyes a mire of confusion and interest.

'Just wait.' He stepped back and rummaged in a bag that was bursting at the seams. He pulled his hand free and handed her a string of golden beads. 'Help me.'

'Help you what?' She countered, her eyes glazed with uncertainty as she took the beads gingerly in her grasp.

'Decorate the tree,' he said with a half-smile as he watched the frost curl along the strand where her fingers touched, turning each bead into a tiny crystal.

She looked up, alarmed. 'I'll ruin them. I'll ruin the tree.'

'No,' Daniel said softly, stepping closer. 'You'll make every decoration better.'

Watching him with interest as her eyes found the array of sparkling reds and golds, beads and tinsel, glass baubles with patterns of snow wrapping around their centres. Her eyes lit up with joy as her mind began working, thinking of how to make the most splendid and beautiful tree with the mismatch of ornaments.

'I'd love to,' she gasped, bending to pick up some tinsel from the floor and wrapping it around her neck like a scarf. Daniel laughed as she spun, the tinsel spiralling around her, making her eyes glow brighter. In that moment, they were not just decorating a tree; they were creating a memory to cherish forever.

Lifting the tall fir tree and placing it at the window in the living room, Daniel secured it at the base in a pot of earth he gathered from the back garden. It stood tall and proud by the window, the curtains pulled back as the low light from the street lamps and the glow of the warm fire lit up its branches in anticipation.

Lumi gathered the boxes and bags filled with the most exquisite decorations, her eyes growing wide at the myriad of colours, the numerous fabrics, and the shiny surfaces that reflected the most enchanting illumination.

The joyful tones of the music now playing softly from the old gramophone, which had been collecting dust in the corner by the piano, and the mulled wine Daniel had prepared added an extra thrill to the festivities. The air became thick with heat and light and the promise of many possibilities.

The room seemed to thrum with energy and joy, and Daniel felt the flickers of warm emotion trail over his skin. *It was love*. Love was filling his cottage despite the years it had been missing.

Together, they looped the garland across the fireplace and the chains of beads around the fir tree's branches. Where her fingers passed, the gold shimmered with frost, each bead transformed into something that caught the firelight like starlight. Candles were collected and displayed around the room, adding warmth and a cosiness that had been absent until tonight.

They moved slowly around the tree, Daniel laughing at the knots of tangled tinsel, Lumi marvelling at the tiny wooden stars and glass baubles. When he pulled out a paper star bent with age, his face grimaced with a tangible emotion of grief.

'My wife and I made this once, long ago. It's clumsy, but… I can't ever throw it away,' he explained.

Lumi touched it gently, her expression tender. 'Then it belongs here still. It should have its place at the top of the tree, a memory to cherish and gaze upon always.' She fastened it carefully on the topmost branch, the frost tracing the edges until it gleamed like new. It sparkled with its own energy, a guiding light illuminating the tree.

At one point, Daniel found himself with a string of lights hopelessly knotted around his arms. Lumi laughed, a sound like bells, and stepped forward to untangle him. Her fingers brushed his shoulders, cool and delicate, and for a moment neither of them moved. The world seemed to pause, wrapped in the glow of firelight and pine.

Finally, they stepped back. The tree blazed—tinsel sparkling, baubles gleaming, frost catching the light in a thousand tiny stars. It was not just a tree, but a symbol of hope and joy for a Christmas yet to come, a sight that filled their hearts with warmth and fulfilment.

'It looks alive,' Daniel whispered.

Lumi's eyes shone, reflecting the glow. 'It looks… like joy.' Her smile widened then as she admired the effort and beautiful creation they had made together.

There was a silence, warm and full, as they stood shoulder to shoulder in the glow of the tree. Then Daniel reached into the final box and lifted a small ornament —a glass heart, cracked along one edge but still intact.

'This goes last,' he said. 'At the centre.' He turned, offering it to her. 'Will you place it?' Hope filled his eyes, and he seemed to hold his breath. This meant the world to him, and Lumi could see that reflected in the slight welling of his gaze.

Her hand trembled as she took it, frost swirling briefly along the glass. She hung it carefully, right at the heart of the tree. The light caught in its facets, scattering across the room. Where the cracks created shadows along the walls, the room looked like every surface had been touched by frost.

When she turned back to him, her expression was soft, unguarded. 'Thank you,' she whispered.

'For what?' He asked with curiosity.

‘For giving me a Christmas.’ Her eyes welled up like she was about to shed glass tears, and his heart could have torn at the emotion of it.

Daniel’s throat tightened. He couldn’t answer—so instead he pulled her gently into his arms, and together they stood before the glowing tree, their heads meeting as they explored every part of the tree they had created.

In the warmth of the room, among the fragmented shadows of frost that caressed every wall, the world outside hushed beneath the falling snow, and inside, their heartbeats fell into a rhythm of their own. In the quiet wonder of that moment, nothing needed to be said.

Chapter Thirteen

A Few Words Shared

After the tree was lit and the last crumbs of mince pies swept from the table, the cottage settled into a soft quiet. Outside, snow fell thick again, muffling the world in white. Inside, the fire crackled low, throwing amber light across the shelves where Daniel's old notebooks sat untouched.

Lumi's gaze drifted there as she curled on the chair opposite him, her silver hair glinting with stray frost. 'Those books,' she asked softly. 'They are yours?'

Daniel followed her eyes, his jaw tightening. 'Old stories. Not worth much now. Some are my own words; others are tales from much-admired authors.'

'I would like to see,' she said, almost a plea. Books had been scarce when she had once been mortal, and those with the ability to read the words were few and far between. Lumi had never been taught how to read, but she remembered with warmth the tales her father would read to her when they were huddled as a family around the hearth.

Reluctantly, he shuffled like he was about to rise, but Lumi stood first and made her way to the bookcase. Her fingers ran across the many spines of the books, the dust collecting at her skin as her frost danced along the worn covers. Finally, her fingers lingered over a battered spine, and, pulling it from the shelf, as if it had called to her, she took it back to the armchair.

Its dark leather cover was cracked from use, and the pages were yellow and worn at the edges. She hesitated before opening it on her lap, as if the paper might burn her.

Lumi turned the pages carefully, her touch leaving a faint halo of frost along the dog-eared pages and worn leather. She gazed at the first few pages of the book, and her breath caught. The scroll was elegant and swirling, like the patterns of her frost. At that moment, she wished she knew what it said.

'I was never taught to read,' she said as a blush rose across her cheeks. The handwriting sprawling across the pages seemed to have been recorded with a kind of eagerness. But the words—those she couldn't understand.

Daniel watched her with deep thought, then gently lifted the book from her hands. 'Then let me tell you a story,' he said, his voice carrying the promise of a transformative journey through the power of words.

His eyes found the page, and his breath hitched, but regaining his composure, he read.

Love is the hearth of the soul. Without it, winter devours us. To hold another's hand is to remind the heart that it is alive. To laugh is to defy the cold. To live is to belong, and belonging is the only true magic the world grants us.

His eyes lifted. A radiance danced across them as though these words finally made sense again and belonged to them.

Her eyes were luminous as she said, 'Daniel… these words. They burn.'

He sat back heavily across from her, rubbing at the back of his neck. 'I wrote that a long time ago, before I lost Clara. Before silence took root in me.'

Lumi stood and knelt before him, and, reaching forward, her finger traced the ink, frost glimmering faintly where she touched. 'You wrote of love as though you knew it deeply.'

'I did,' he whispered. His voice roughened. 'And when it was gone, I had nothing left to say.'

For a long moment, the only sound was the fire's sigh, a gentle crackling and popping that seemed to echo the emotions in the room. The room held its breath as the moment turned into minutes. Then Daniel turned another page and read aloud again.

To cherish someone is to catch snow before it melts—to hold something fleeting is to call it eternal.

His voice was quiet, awed, and the words seemed to weave themselves back into the room, breathing warmth into walls that had long been dark and bare.

Daniel closed his eyes. He hadn't read those words in years, hadn't let himself. And now, hearing them in her presence, he felt them strike somewhere deep, like embers stirred back into flame.

When he opened his eyes again, she was watching him. 'The man who wrote this,' she said, 'is still here. His words are not gone. Only waiting to be let free again.'

Something in his chest broke open, and for a moment, he thought he might weep. His words had been so full of love, a blessing he had received from his wife. As the tears threatened to fall, he took a shuddering breath and let his gaze linger on the flames.

His mind was filled with opposing emotions. Grief, on one hand, danced with healing on the other. He reached across the space between them, covering her cheek with his palm. Her skin was winter, his was summer, but between them the book lay open, bridging the years between who he had been and who he might still become.

'Perhaps the words will fall freely again,' he said softly, 'I think I've been waiting for something, or someone to bring those words back.'

Lumi watched him intently, his gaze back on the flames, and her lips curved into a smile, fragile and luminous. 'Then let us read more of them together.'

And so they did, nestled together on the sofa, the firelight pooling golden around them, the old words of love reborn on his lips. In this shared experience, the cottage seemed less hollow than it ever had. Daniel felt—for the first time in years—that he would no longer be writing alone. That his words could again be shared and freely heard in the quiet world around them.

Chapter Fourteen

Before the Frost

They had been reading quietly for some time when Daniel noticed Lumi's eyes had grown distant, the book open in her lap but somehow forgotten. Her gaze seemed to look beyond the fire, beyond the cottage itself, as if into another world or another time.

'What is it?' he asked gently.

She hesitated, her lips parting, then closing again, like the words were on her tongue but unable to leave her lips. She shivered as though her own frost had chilled her, but at last, she whispered, 'I was remembering… who I was, before.'

'Before the frost? Before the bargain?' He whispered, eyes fixed on hers.

Her silver eyes lifted to his. 'Yes. Before the bargain. Before winter devoured everything.'

She shifted in her chair, her hands folded in her lap, across the pages of the book, and for a moment she almost seemed younger—more fragile, more mortal.

'I was a girl in a small village,' she said slowly, as though tugging threads loose from a tapestry. 'Not noble, not remarkable. Just… alive. My father tended the fields, my mother spun wool. I had two brothers, always covered in mud, always laughing. And a sister, Leira. She was younger — much younger — just a babe, with hair like summer wheat. I would braid it for her each morning, though she never sat still long enough.'

A faint smile touched her lips.

'I loved the river most. When the days were long and the air was warm, my brothers and I would slip away from the work and plunge into its waters, our laughter carrying across the fields. We told stories while gathering berries and sang while mending clothes. Life was simple, but it was ours.' Her eyes were warm with the memories.

But then her smile faded. 'On the harvest festival, we would dance in the square. I remember the feel of earth under my bare feet, the music of pipes and drums, the lanterns swinging in the night. I remember thinking it would always be so. That there would always be laughter, and song, and warmth.'

She fell silent, her hands tightening together. The memories were warm, but the pain of recalling those days of her youth was stirring up a grief she had not felt in years. Frost shattered across the book below her hands, encasing it in shards of ice.

Daniel leaned forward, his voice quiet. 'And you lost it. You lost your family. That is a hard cross to bear.'

Her gaze snapped to him, sharp and full of sorrow. 'I lost *everything*. The fields went barren. The river froze. Laughter turned to silence. My sister's braids came loose, and her hair grew brittle as straw. By the time I made the bargain, I could hardly remember what her laughter sounded like.'

Daniel's throat tightened. He wanted to reach for her, to hold her sorrow in his arms, but he held back, sensing she needed the words to flow unbroken.

'People remember me now only as frost,' she said, her voice trembling. 'A shadow, a blessing whispered over windows. But I was once a daughter. A sister. A girl who loved to swim in the river, who stained her hands red with berries, who danced until her feet ached. And no one remembers her now but me.'

Tears strained at her eyes, glistening like ice in the corners, sharp and stinging like they would tear her apart.

Tears also pricked Daniel's eyes before he could stop them. He leaned across the space between them and caught her hands in his, warm against cold.

'I'll remember her,' he said fiercely. 'I'll remember all of it. The river, the songs, the dancing. I'll remember for you.'

Her breath hitched, and for the first time, the glass-like tears melted and glittered in her silver eyes. 'That is the greatest gift you could give me.'

The shattered ice on the pages of the book in her lap dissolved and disappeared. Daniel's words gazed up at her, smooth and elegant, perfect and unscathed. She sighed, relieved that her sorrow had not shattered his words or his expression of love. His book was filled with promises of the past, and yet there was hope for his future.

He slipped closer, gripping her hands tighter in his. 'I'll not only remember those memories for you, but I will remember our memories too. I will remember the vision in white, who lingered before me, her frost blessing doors as I lifted my gaze and looked up. I will remember the joy of the ice rink and the look on your face as you tasted the ice cream.' He smiled, and her gaze softened on his.

'I'll remember the mess of the kitchen as we baked Christmas treats. I'll remember the joy of decorating the tree. But most of all, I will remember the words we shared… my words that are now ready to be written, of the wondrous Christmas gift I received when frost met flame.' He blushed then; his eyes filled with emotion so raw and sincere. He meant every word, and if she left at dawn and he never saw her again, those memories would forever be held in his heart.

She stilled, her heart picking up pace as she felt the honesty of those words, those memories he promised to hold dear. She wouldn't cease to exist or be forgotten come dawn, but her perfect night with the stranger in the snow would live on in his mind and forever in her heart.

For a long time, they stayed like that, holding one another across the sofa, the fire burning low. And in that moment, Lumi didn't feel like frost or spirit. She didn't feel like a forgotten memory or a sacrifice. She felt like a mortal woman, whole and loved, her past and present still alive in the heart of another.

Chapter Fifteen

A Breaking Dawn

The fire had burned low again, a steady bed of embers glowing faintly in the hearth. Daniel sat on the rug, his back against the sofa, while Lumi lingered by the window. Her hand rested lightly on the glass, as frost spiralled outward from her touch in delicate, curling patterns. Her mind was elsewhere as her thoughts wandered, melding with the frost and creating a cold, gilded cage around her.

The clock ticked steadily toward dawn. The clamour of that second-hand ticking was a sound that filled Daniel's ears and head with nervous anxiety. He couldn't unhear it, no matter how hard he tried to focus on other, more enjoyable things.

He watched her in silence, trying to memorise everything—the shimmer in her hair, the way her gaze softened when she thought he wasn't looking. Her starlit eyes and her full, violet lips. The way the fur-lined hood hugged her delicate neck. The frost that perpetually lingered at her fingertips and delicately laced every surface she touched. A part of him already feared that when the sun rose, she would be gone, and all of this would feel like a dream.

'You're quiet,' she said at last, her voice no more than a whisper. Her eyes were large, filled with sudden sadness, and his heart broke at the sight of them.

'I'm trying not to waste a single second,' Daniel admitted. 'Every moment with you feels… fleeting. I want to remember every detail.'

Her shoulders stiffened slightly. She didn't turn. 'It is fleeting. I don't have much time left.'

Something in his chest cracked at the certainty in her tone. It was possibly the most distressing situation he had ever encountered. She no longer had a choice. No free will. Her life was in the hands of something or someone much stronger. 'Tell me,' he said. 'All of it. What happens when the sun comes up?' His voice trembled with the weight of their impending separation.

She let out a slow breath that frosted the windowpane. A shudder ran over her body, as if she was feeling the cold settle in her bones for the first time in centuries.

'The bargain I made binds me to the frost. My body is no longer my own—it belongs to the winter, to the cold spirits of longer nights. Each year, I return only for this one night, to bless, to walk unseen, alone in my duties. When dawn comes, I vanish back into the frost, hidden until the next winter calls me again.'

Daniel's fists tightened in his lap. 'And if you don't go back? What if you decide to stay?'

Her head bowed slightly. 'Then I will unravel. The Goddess of Winter, Cailleach, will not forgive. I will be banished forever from either realm and fade into nothing.'

The words fell heavy between them, like the hush before a storm. The room suddenly felt cold, and there seemed to be a great distance between them as she pulled her gaze away from his. Daniel's eyes were wide with understanding. She would cease to exist if she broke her bargain.

Daniel rose and crossed to her side. 'But is that a life? Centuries of solitude, walking unseen, blessing people who never even know you exist? You've given up everything—your home, your family, your chance to belong. For one night? For what? For duty?' His voice was filled with the pain of understanding, of realising the depth of her sacrifice and the strength of her love.

She turned to him then, eyes flashing like shards of ice. 'For life. For their lives. My choice saved them, Daniel. And my choice keeps their descendants safe to this day. It is no small thing. I have been a saviour to mortals for many centuries.'

His voice softened. 'But what about you? Don't you deserve to be saved, too? You have given up so much and had everyone you loved taken from you. When do you have the life back that you sacrificed?'

The fight in her expression faltered. For a moment, she only looked at him, raw and unguarded. 'I have told myself for centuries that my loneliness was the price of their joy. That it was enough. But tonight…' Her voice broke, barely audible. '…tonight, I am not certain. I'm not sure anymore.'

Daniel cupped her face in his hands, his palms warm against her chill. ‘Then stay even if it’s only for one Christmas. Even if it costs everything. Stay with me.’

Her breath hitched. The frost on the window shivered and cracked, as though reflecting her inner turmoil, the battle between duty and desire, between the life she had and the life she could have.

‘You don’t understand,’ she whispered. ‘If I stay, I will be gone forever. There will be no next winter, no returning. I’ll never see you again, and I will only exist in eternal silence.’

Daniel shook his head. ‘Then I’ll make my own bargain. I’ll pray for your release from this oath you took. I’d rather have one night with you than a lifetime without you. And if silence is the price… well, then… I’ll take your place and remember you loudly, every day I live in the silence waiting for Christmas Eve.’

Lumi’s body stilled, like she was questioning why he would do this for her. Her eyes filled with something fragile and fierce all at once—fear, longing, hope. She pressed her forehead lightly to his, her voice trembling like breaking ice.

‘I can’t ask you to do that. I am so afraid. I can’t ask you to give up your life. Sacrifice yourself for me.’

She gasped, sudden realisation waking within her that she had experienced her first real connection in many years. The warmth she had found in Daniel was returned, with a fierce need to protect and save her.

'I am scared too,' Daniel murmured. 'But I live my life in solitude anyway. I see no one and have lived this way for many years. That's how I know it's worth it, to have you with me a little longer and give you the existence you deserve.'

The window shimmered with a low golden light as the first pale line of dawn edged the horizon outside. It weaved into the room, casting a thin shadow of their bodies against the wall.

Daniel looked at how their shadows fitted together, their bodies melting into one. The frost patterns on the glass flared brightly, pulling his eyes to the breaking dawn, as the delicately laced frost on the window glowed warm for a heartbeat before melting.

Lumi closed her eyes and whispered, 'Then let it be so. I'll stay, but you will make no bargain. If you would sacrifice your life for me, then I can do the same.' Her eyes traced their shadows too, a smile tugging at the merging of their existence.

Daniel wrapped Lumi in a forceful embrace, his arms bound tightly around her. He'd hold on to her and not let go. She would give up the little existence she had to remain with him a little longer, but he would not have that be the end of her story. He'd made up his mind. When the Goddess called her home, he would get down on his knees and pray to Cailleach. He'd beg and bargain with her to release Lumi and let her live the life she deserved.

He'd happily take her place and become a spirit of winter, completing her duties each Christmas Eve. And if that meant he could only see her once every year, even at a distance, that would be enough. Her happiness and opportunity to live would keep his heart warm whilst he waited in the shadows for winter to return.

Chapter Sixteen

Love Against Frost

The horizon blushed faintly gold, streaks of pink, violet and silver seeping into the indigo night sky. Daniel's cottage was hushed, but the world outside seemed to hold its breath as the first light of day reached for the earth.

A cold lingered in the room, the fire having dwindled further, and Daniel could feel the frost nip at his fingers and toes. The sun would rise soon and release the frost's grip, and that felt like a burden he could not carry.

She'd be gone forever if he didn't make his bargain and soon.

Lumi stood in the centre of the room, her form shimmering faintly, as though her body were made of frost and starlight instead of flesh. She was beautiful, even as her essence faded and each flicker of sunrise tugged at her, and she began to fade. The very threads of her essence unspooling into the air in light, crisp fragments of ice.

Daniel clutched her hands tightly. 'Fight it,' he urged. 'Stay with me.'

Her voice trembled. 'The frost is calling. It does not release what it claims easily.'

'Then don't listen to it. Listen to me. To this.' He pressed her cold palm against his chest, where his heart beat steadily and desperate. 'You don't belong to the frost anymore. You belong here.'

Her eyes shimmered with tears that froze before they could fall. She closed her fingers, feeling the warmth of his heartbeat beneath her hand, and as her gaze met Daniel's, he smiled and pulled his hand away. Surprised by the abrupt release of his warmth, she stilled as Daniel got down on his knees, his head now level with her fading fingers.

'What are you doing?' she gasped, realisation bursting within her. 'Please don't do this. Don't make me carry this burden,' she urged. For a moment, her form flickered more brightly, a glow of silver fire.

'I must. You have been bound to winter for too long. Let me do this for you… for the sacrifice you made.' He closed his eyes then and refused to hear her pleas. Her hands reached for him, but he remained still, as though he had become a statue; she couldn't reach his internal mind.

Suddenly, his lips parted, and the words flowed. Lumi froze, and her skin prickled with dread as the words were cast into the brightening room.

'Goddess Cailleach, please hear my prayer. I have met the most amazing being, a spirit of your winter, and I have opened my lonely heart to her. She has made the loneliness I carried bearable. She has given me one night of utter bliss, and I wish to make a bargain for her life… her soul.' Daniel shuddered, his eyes closing tighter as he took a steadying breath and continued.

'She deserves more. She should live as a mortal, surrounded by love and family. I make this bargain…' Lumi gripped his shoulder, her head shaking furiously as the words continued to spill. He ignored her touch. He ignored the words she now spoke fiercely, begging him to stop.

'Let me take her place. Let me carry her burden. Let me be the spirit of winter who serves you, not her. She has done her duty. She deserves all that she has earned.' His shoulders sagged and his head lowered, eyes still shut as he wondered if it was enough. *Did the Cailleach hear him?*

But then the light of dawn streamed fuller through the windows, striking Lumi like a tide. Her body wavered. Wisps of frost lifted from her skin, swirling toward the air as her figure began to be engulfed by a storm of ice and snow. It swirled vigorously around her, Lumi trapped in a blizzard, her body fading.

'*No!* Daniel cried, reaching through spiralling snow, ice and shards that threatened to bite into his skin. He pulled her close, as though he could anchor her by sheer will. 'You can not have her. Please!' he begged as his tears dampened her shoulder, hot against her chill. 'I can't lose you. Not now.'

Lumi gasped softly, her voice breaking. 'Daniel…'

And then, something shifted. The warmth that had lingered from the ebbing coals sputtered and died as a bright light flashed, encasing the room. Frost found every corner, every surface, as the room stilled, as if it were frozen in time.

The frost patterns on the windows shivered and cracked—not with cold, but with expectation, as though they were waiting for their master to arrive.

A light, like the brightest star in the sky, had found its way into the room and blinded Daniel for a moment. He stood, clinging tighter to Lumi, her edges fraying.

A voice whispered, yet powerfully met their ears. 'Who calls me with their prayer?' The breath of a chill pressed closer, growing colder as the light softened, and a figure appeared.

At once, they were not alone. A towering yet ethereal figure stood before them. Her skin was as blue as smooth, cool glass, as if she had been forged from the ice of heaven. Her hair was white, long and moved with the energy of soft, feathered snow. Her eyes seemed to hold the winter, a flurry of blue and white with a penetrating gaze that could have the observer frozen in place. The room around her seemed to shift and move in her presence. Then it settled as her eyes found them.

'It was you. I heard your prayer,' she said smoothly, her eyes fixed on Daniel. 'You dare to make a bargain with winter?' She said with an icy smile.

'It is true. I prayed for your presence. I wish to make a bargain. Her soul for mine.' He said flatly but with conviction, returning the cold smile.

She looked at him with curiosity. Then her eyes found Lumi's. 'Are you unhappy in your duty? Do you not receive fulfilment in knowing the people you bless, receive the winter's favour?'

Lumi shrank under her gaze, her fingers lacing with Daniel's to find her strength. 'I am happy. There was no need for you to make this journey. I wish to return to my duties.'

'No!' Daniel said fearfully, his arm lacing around Lumi's waist. 'She wishes to stay, and I vow to take her place. Her soul for mine. I will be her bargain.'

The fire in the hearth leapt high, roaring brighter than it should have. *Had he angered the Goddess?* But as he looked at Lumi, where his warmth touched her, the frost binding her seemed to weaken.

'It is done,' Cailleach said. Her eyes bore a darker shade of steel. 'The bargain is made.'

Lumi's body steadied, flickering less. She stared at him in wonder. 'Your fire… it holds me.'

'No,' Daniel whispered, tightening his hold. 'It's your mortality. It is binding you to this realm, to the heat, the fire. It's yours to embrace. Frost and flame, together. The life you deserve.'

The Goddess stilled as her face looked like it might shatter, just as a wide smile graced her appearance. 'No,' she said coldly. 'It is not for her to embrace.'

'You can't take her. My bargain? You said it was done. Take me, not her. Please!' Daniel's voice was strained with emotion, his heart hammering in his chest as his eyes filled with cold, shrill tears.

'I can't take you. I can't take either of you.' She folded her arms loosely over her chest, her eyes brightening as a warmth grew there.

'I observe all my spirits in their duties. I see how the world moves around them, like they are shadows of the winter sun, ignored and unheard. I watched you, Lumi. I watched you open your heart to a mortal who was just as lonely as you have been. And it warmed me,' she laughed lightly. 'It warmed me… the Goddess of Winter and I couldn't pull my eyes away.'

'It is endearing that a heart so lonely would see a spirit that was never meant to be observed by mortals. And yet you saw her. She also saw you, Daniel, and the world through your eyes. It moved me, which is no easy feat. And I felt compelled to offer my own blessing.' She took a step toward them, her eyes filled with a hint of gold as her skin reflected the early morning sun.

Her fingertips gently rested upon a shoulder of each of the beings before her, and as her frost spilt over their bodies, caressing them in a shimmer of blue, she stepped back. 'It is done!'

Outside, the sun broke free of the horizon. Light poured into the cottage, golden and fierce. For one suspended heartbeat, Lumi arched against it—caught between vanishing and staying. The frosted tendril that had seemed to envelop the cottage lifted, coiling in the air into small, light particles before disappearing in a white flash. The Goddess was gone, too.

Then Lumi cried out, a sound like ice fracturing and bells ringing all at once, and the frost binding her shattered. It disappeared into the remnants of the cold void that had flashed, and all at once the room was bathed in heat, the fire flaring gently as the warmth met Lumi's cheeks.

Silver sparks scattered across the room, dissolving into nothing. When the glow dimmed, Lumi stood solid, honest, breathless in Daniel's arms. Her skin still cool, but no longer fading. Her heartbeat fluttered beneath his own—fragile but alive.

She looked up at him, wide-eyed. 'I… I'm still here. And so are you!'

Daniel laughed through tears, pulling her closer. 'You're here. You're really here. You have been granted a blessing and you can stay!'

Lumi buried her face against his shoulder, her whole body trembling with relief. 'The bargain is broken, and no other was needed.'

He kissed her hair, then her temple, then finally her lips—this time not with desperation, but with the fierce joy of belonging. The overwhelming happiness that grew within him left his heart soaring and his chest warm.

Outside, the snow caught the dawn and sparkled like a million diamonds. Winter was still winter, but inside the little cottage, warmth and frost had found each other—and neither would ever again walk alone.

Chapter Seventeen

Christmas Morning

The cottage smelled of cinnamon and woodsmoke. Morning light spilt golden across the worn floorboards, glittering where it touched the frosted flowers that still lingered faintly on the windows. They no longer pulsed with binding magic—only with memory.

Daniel stirred the porridge on the stove, humming under his breath. He wasn't much of a cook, but he'd found dried fruit in the cupboard and a little jar of honey.

Somehow, making breakfast felt sacred—like an offering to the day, to the new life unfolding.

Behind him, Lumi laughed softly. The sound still startled him with its beauty, like bells in snow.

'You hum off-key,' she teased, standing barefoot by the hearth. Her hair tumbled loose over her shoulders, silver catching the sunlight, and she looked more alive than he had ever seen her.

He turned, mock-offended. 'Do I? I thought I was improving.'

'You are,' she admitted, crossing the room with that unearthly grace of hers. 'But still off-key.'

Daniel handed her a steaming bowl. 'Then you'll have to teach me.'

She accepted it, fingers brushing his. Warmth lingered where they touched, a miracle in itself. They sat together at the little table, sharing the simple meal. Outside, the town stirred awake—distant bells chimed, children's laughter rang across the snow, and a choir's voices drifted faintly through the crisp air.

Lumi listened with wide eyes, as though each sound was a gift. ‘So, this is Christmas morning,’ she murmured.

‘This is Christmas morning,’ Daniel confirmed, smiling. ‘Messy, noisy, sweet. Full of life.’

She reached across the table, taking his hand. ‘It feels like… home.’

His chest tightened with a swell of joy so fierce it almost hurt. ‘That’s because it is.’

For a while, they sat in silence, watching the snow sparkle outside the window. The world was the same as it had always been—cold, imperfect, alive. But for the first time in centuries, Lumi belonged to it.

And Daniel, who had thought his heart too broken for joy, found it full again.

The door suddenly rapped with urgency, and stilling, Daniel felt his heart still. For a brief moment, he thought he would awaken from this incredible dream, but as his eyes gazed at Lumi, real and mortal before him, he slowly stood and made his way to the door.

Opening it slowly, snow drifting in as the laughter of Christmas morning flowed into the room, Daniel's eyes fell on the small frame of Matthew.

'Merry Christmas, Mr Hale,' he said with a blush forming on his cold cheeks. The snow clung to his mittens, and his woollen hat was flaked with soft, light flecks of ice.

'Merry Christmas to you, too, Matthew,' Daniel returned warmly, the smile etched across his face caught Matthew off guard. He had never seen Mr Hale smile… ever.

'I just thought I would call around to invite you to Christmas dinner. My mother said she has prepared too much and wondered if you'd like to join us? You know, so you aren't alone on Christmas day.' Matthew's eyes, filled with emotion, gripped Daniel's with need. A need Daniel couldn't understand.

'Is everything okay, Matthew?' he questioned, concern growing for the young man who lingered at his door, eyes full of worry.

'I just… well, you see,' he shuffled on the spot, his eyes finding his feet. 'Well, I see you often on your own, and I worry you might be lonely. I don't want you to spend this day on your own,' he said sincerely.

Daniel's gaze softened. 'Please come inside. There is someone I'd like you to meet.'

Matthew hesitated, his face marred with confusion, but he entered cautiously as his eyes found the tree. 'Your tree is beautiful,' he said honestly.

'It is,' Daniel replied. 'I had a little help putting it together.'

Eyes wide and full of awe, Matthew's gaze rested on the incredible sight before him. Hair spun of silver and dressed in the finest dress, which resembled winter itself, the most beautiful woman stood at the arch near the kitchen, her eyes filled with joy.

'And who might you be?' she asked with words that would warm the coldest heart.

'I'm Matthew. Who are you?' Matthew whispered.

'I'm Lumi,' the striking woman said as she stepped forward and offered Matthew her hand. He took it and shook it hesitantly, noting the cool touch of her skin, even through his mittens, like she had been playing in the snow all morning.

'Tell your mother we would be honoured to celebrate Christmas with you and share a meal with your wonderful family,' Lumi beamed. Matthew smiled shyly, looking to Daniel, who just nodded his acceptance of the invitation.

With a heart full of joy, Matthew dashed towards the door. He paused, turning back to them with a delighted smile. 'I'm off to tell my mother about our dinner guests,' he announced, his excitement palpable. His gaze lingered on Mr Hale and Lumi, a smile stretching across his face as he saw them together.

As Daniel and Lumi watched, Matthew sprinted down the path from the cottage, his eyes shining with a magical light. 'My wish has come true!' he shouted, his voice filled with joy as he took off toward his home.

Daniel and Lumi slowly closed the door, their minds confused by Matthew's last statement, but shrugging, they moved back to the fireside to finish the remains of their hot cocoa.

Later, they stepped outside together. The villagers bustled past, smiling in greeting, unaware of the miracle that had unfolded in the little cottage. Lumi tightened her scarf against the cold, her cheeks touched with rose. Daniel slipped his arm around her, and she leaned in without hesitation.

Snowflakes drifted down, catching in her hair like tiny crowns. She tilted her face to the sky and whispered, as though to the world itself:

'Thank you.'

Daniel pressed a kiss to her temple, smiling into her silver hair. 'Merry Christmas, Lumi.'

Her hand tightened in his. 'Merry Christmas, Daniel.'

As the bells rang out across the town, Daniel and Lumi walked forward together, their hearts full of love and warmth. They were no longer alone, but a united pair, ready to embrace the joy of Christmas.

The warmth lingered between them, as the frost nipped at their noses, and Daniel held Lumi a little closer as they took the path to Matthew's home. Inside the house, the atmosphere was warm, with lights and decorations, and a fire that burned brightly in the hearth.

The table was a sight to behold, a testament to the warmth and joy of the season. Lumi felt a sense of belonging as she took in the beautiful scene, grateful to be part of the celebration, no longer a whisper in the shadows but a cherished part of the family.

Matthew greeted them both warmly as they settled in front of the hearth, sipping mulled wine whilst being regaled by Matthew's father with fanciful stories of wonderful Christmas celebrations and the joy of opening presents on early Christmas morning.

Sliding his hand under the tree, Matthew produced the most perfect little gift box and handed it to Lumi. It was carelessly wrapped, the bow askew on top, but it was beautiful, she thought, as she looked at Matthew.

'What is this?' she asked with wonder.

'It's a gift for you,' he smiled. 'For making Mr Hale so very happy this Christmas.'

Gently tearing the paper and revealing a little cardboard box, she pulled the top off and dared to look inside. Her pulse quickened as she gazed upon its contents.

Lying at the bottom, the red thread looped around the top of the most precious glass bauble. It was a little scratched in places, but the light reflected an item inside.

Looking up as her eyes found Matthew's, Lumi opened her mouth to speak, but the words failed to leave her lips.

'I have hung this bauble on the tree every year, but today, after I returned from Mr Hale's house, my eyes fell upon this when I returned home. I instantly thought of you and wanted you to have it,' Matthew blushed as Lumi gazed back at the gift.

Behind the scratched glass, standing in the centre, coated in soft white feathers that resembled snow, was the most radiant snowflake. Simple but beautiful, it reminded Lumi of what she had been.

Her eyes yet again met Matthews. 'Thank you,' she whispered. 'I have never had a gift this wonderful.'

Pulling his eyes to Daniel, Matthew continued, 'I asked Winter for a wish, and that wish came true. I want you to have a little bit of winter, so you'll always remember the joy you brought to Mr Hale.'

Chapter Eighteen

Christmas For The Fated

The once-quiet, lifeless cottage at the edge of town had undergone a miraculous transformation. No longer shrouded in darkness and cold, it now radiated with light and warmth, a beacon of hope and joy against the backdrop of the dark forest—a true testament to the magic of the holiday season.

On Christmas Eve, its windows blazed with golden light; the roof was crowned in twinkling garlands, and wreaths hung from every door and shutter. From the chimney, smoke curled in a fragrant ribbon of pine and spice. Children's laughter spilt into the snowy night, mingling with the jingling of bells tied to the old wooden sledges by the porch.

Inside, the house was a wonderland. Paper stars hung from the beams. Holly and ivy twined across the mantelpiece, where stockings bulged with secrets. The great tree stood proudly by the window, so laden with baubles, ribbons, and frosted ornaments that it seemed to bow under the weight of joy itself.

Standing in the doorway, Daniel's heart swelled with joy as he beheld the festive scene. His hair may have turned silver, but his smile was as bright as ever, a reflection of the love and togetherness he now experienced. Christmas was no longer a time of silence and absence, but a vibrant celebration of life and love.

Across the room, Lumi bent over a tray of gingerbread, guiding two small hands as they pressed sugar-dusted shapes onto the cookies. Her hair was still silver, but her eyes glowed with the light of a woman who had chosen life. She glanced up, meeting Daniel's gaze, and for an instant the years fell away—the spark of frost, the blaze of fire—still there, still theirs.

One of the children ran to him, mittened hands tugging at his sleeve. 'Papa, come hang the star!'

Daniel laughed, hoisting the boy onto his shoulders, guiding them to the topmost branch of the tall pine tree. Together, they placed the glowing star ornament atop, and a cheer rose from the whole room.

'Another fine Christmas, father,' Matthew said, as he approached the pair at the tree. A grown man with a family of his own, Matthew had been named after the young boy who had made his Christmas wish all those years ago. Daniel and Lumi had been blessed with their own children: Matthew, who arrived two Christmases later, and Clara, two summers after that.

They had completed their family and lived a cherished life, happy and loved in their small cottage by the woods. Life had been good to Matthew and Clara, each being blessed with a family and children of their own.

As was their cherished tradition, they returned home every Christmas Eve. Daniel and Lumi welcomed their children and grandchildren with the warmth and joy of Christmas, their small dining room table seeming to expand with the abundance of love.

When the children had tumbled back to their games, Daniel crossed to Lumi. She pressed a sugared kiss to his cheek, cool and sweet all at once. Watching their children laugh as they shared memories by the fire, while their grandchildren were engaged in festive games, Lumi squeezed Daniel a little tighter.

'Do you remember,' she murmured, 'our first Christmas Eve? How empty the house was?'

'I do,' he said softly, cupping her face. 'And how you filled it with the love and joy that had been missing.'

She leaned into his touch, her eyes bright. 'Every year since has been ours, Daniel. And every year to come will be too.'

The door swung open vigorously, the cold being dragged in as a gentleman entered, a woman's hand gripped in his and a sullen teenager at their backs. The gentleman's warm eyes landed on Lumi and Daniel, and his grin widened into the warmest smile.

'Has it really been a year since we last saw each other?' he questioned as Daniel stepped forward and shook his hand warmly. Lumi raced forward, pushing in between Daniel and the hand he still firmly gripped. Throwing her hand around the gentleman's shoulders, she welcomed him warmly.

'Matthew. It has been too long, but I am so glad you could join us again this Christmas,' she said with joy as she gripped him tighter.

'Wouldn't miss it for the world,' Matthew said as his eyes found the children, splayed out on the rug by the hearth. 'Mark, why don't you join the children. Maybe you'll find some Christmas spirit,' he laughed as his eyes found his son's. In typical teenage fashion, Mark rolled his eyes but did as his father bade.

Matthew's eyes found the gloriously decorated tree as his gaze settled on a glass bauble, scuffed but glittering. 'You still have it?' he asked, his eyes filled with emotion.

Lumi smiled and gripped his arm. 'Of course! I told you all those years ago, it was the most wonderful gift I'd ever received.' Their eyes gazed upon that bauble, the snowflake glimmering within and their hearts melted at the sight of it.

Lumi reached for Mary, 'It's wonderful to see you again.' Taking her hand, she led Mary to the kitchen, where a few mugs of mulled wine lingered on the sideboard.

Around them, the house pulsed with life—family, and friends drawn in by warmth and tradition. A choir sang down the lane, children darted through the halls with ribbons, and in every corner, candles glowed.

The house was no longer a symbol of loneliness or a prison for a frost-bound spirit. It was now a sanctuary of love and belonging, a home filled with the warmth of the fire and the beauty of the frost, a true embodiment of the Christmas spirit.

As sunset neared, Daniel slipped an arm around Lumi's waist. The children were nestled on the rug, waiting for stories before bed. She kissed his temple and whispered, 'Christmas Eve is ours now. To love. To cherish. To remember that fate gave us more than a single night.'

Daniel nodded, his heart overflowing. 'To forever.'

With the tree ablaze, the stockings full, and the house alive with laughter, they began their Christmas together. It was a moment of fate, of choice, and of never facing another Christmas alone again. The warmth of the scene enveloped them, a reminder that they were part of something special, something that would last forever.

Epilogue

The Promise of Love

Turning slowly, unseen and unheard as he gently placed his delicate frost across the door of the small cottage, on the edge of the woods in this delightful wee town, Frasier lingered a moment longer. The sound of laughter, the promise of love and warmth forever, swirled around his senses as he stood motionless at the door.

His duty was simple: walk and visit every home within the town and grace each door with the gift of winter, a blessing to bestow on the mortals who needed a little hope, love, or to lift the bleakness of the colder nights. But this house seemed different. It had once been marred in shadow; he could feel the lingering memories of its cold, dark, lonely heart, now filled with love, yet still echoing what it was before.

Stepping toward the light blazing through the window, he dared to look inside, and there his heart stilled as he watched a family who cherished each other, filling Christmas with love and light. His heart ached for a moment, his mind flooded with memories of his own past. It may have been centuries since he last felt like he belonged, but those feelings lingered somewhere deep within him.

As he observed the celebrations, his memories felt suddenly fresh and real, as if they had just resurfaced and had been hidden in his heart all this time. It shocked him into silence as his heart ached for what he had once had.

He watched a moment longer, and with a smile across his face, he slowly edged down the path, heading into town. He touched a few more doors as he made his way toward the square, when suddenly he heard the most angelic voice, which drew him closer.

There, beneath the glow of the finely decorated, glittering tall pine tree, sat a young woman, wrapped in a woollen coat, her scarf tugged tight around her neck and her hands cold in the drifting snow. He stilled as he beheld her. Her beauty was ethereal, a stark contrast to the melancholy in her eyes and the loneliness that surrounded her.

Frasier couldn't pull his eyes away. He was drawn to that sombre song and the beautiful face of the young woman who carried it to his ears. She couldn't see him, even though in that moment he longed for her to. To sit with her for a moment to briefly relieve her grief would be a pleasure if it released her pain.

He closed his eyes, caught up in the melancholy notes, his heart beating faster as her pain reached for the stars. Frost glittered around her, drawn to her sadness. As her words stopped and his eyes opened, he was startled when her gaze fell on him.

He took a step back, as though to flee and disappear back into the night, but she stood, her heart in her throat as she spoke.

'Wait!' She called out. 'Who are you?' she gasped, her eyes wide and filled with curiosity.

He stilled, his heart beating so fast that he felt it might burst out of his chest; then, slowly, he turned and looked upon her face. The surprise in her eyes was evident, a sign of the unexpected turn their Christmas was about to take. It was a moment that left her intrigued and eager to know more.

The sadness and longing that had been held there seemed to have lifted somewhat, and now she looked at him with hope, to the promise of something new. His presence had brought a glimmer of joy to her eyes, a stark contrast to the loneliness and despair he had just witnessed.

'Would you like to join me for a hot cocoa?' She blushed as she took a step toward him. 'It would be such a pity for us both to be out here on our own this Christmas.'

Eyes widening, skin tingling and feeling an urge to step toward her warmth, Frasier took a steadying breath.

'I'd like that,' he said, his voice filled with emotion he hadn't experienced in centuries. 'The cocoa will only freeze when I touch it, but I'd be happy to sit with you a wee while longer.'

Enjoying my Cosy Christmas Romantic Fantasy**, Frost and Flame**?

Why not check out my other titles:

Books 1 and 2 of **The Blood and Power series** are available now, and book three will be the last instalment of this Scottish fantasy series, released next year (2026).

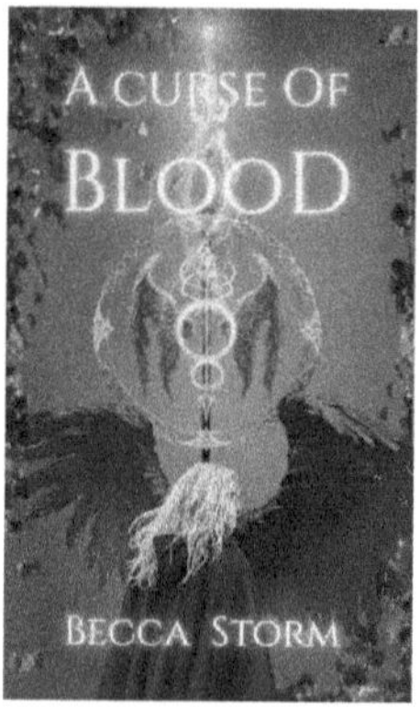

A Dark Versus Light Portal Fantasy based on Scottish and Celtic Mythology

An impossible dream. A shattered heart. A fantasy too real to escape.

When a heartbroken young woman, trapped in a mundane life, is thrust into a fantastical realm eerily reminiscent of the stories she once used to escape her pain, she must confront ancient magic, unexpected destiny, and the truth about who she really is—before the curse binding her new world consumes them both.

The Power and Blood series is a stirring journey of self-discovery, heartbreak, and magic—a tale for anyone who's ever longed to escape and found something extraordinary waiting on the other side.

The Triquetra Series

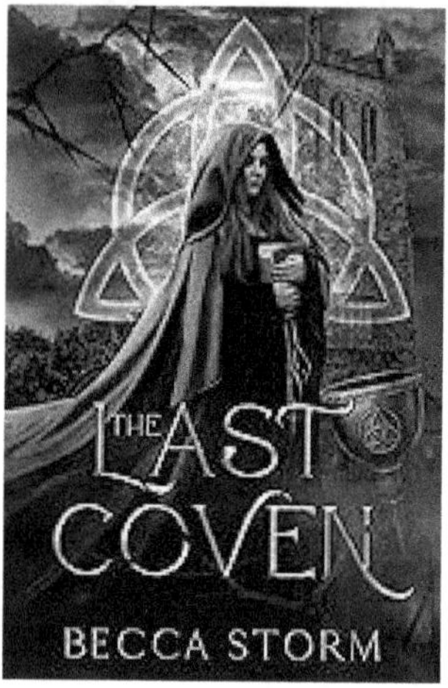

The Last Coven (Historical fiction set in 1650, Kilwinning, Ayrshire, Scotland). At the height of the witchcraft trials, this novel features a blend of real-life women and fictional characters and details the horrific persecution, arrests, and torture these women faced at the hands of the Presbyterian church. In their drive to root out all evil and create a society driven by Godliness, the acts committed by the church were more evil than any crime any of these women, and some men, were accused of. Discover their fate and that of their coven **in The Last Coven.**

Follow the outcome of the earlier 1618 witchcraft trials in Irvine, Ayrshire, Scotland. In this prequel to The Last Coven, the second book in the series, **A Coven Lost**, well-known local figures are featured among those accused and tried for witchcraft. See what becomes of their coven in A Coven Lost. (Due to be released July 2025)

The Cherry Blossom Series

When grief threatens to consume her, Deana retreats to the one place that still feels like home—beneath the cherry blossom tree of her childhood. But sorrow doesn't keep her grounded for long. An unexpected encounter with a mysterious force pulls her into a world where ancient Scottish folklore pulses just beneath the surface of reality.

Bound by emotion and mystery, Deana is thrust into a journey of self-discovery—and into the arms of Havard, a man as enigmatic as the secrets he keeps. As the line between the seen and unseen blurs, Deana must navigate a tangled path of love, loss, and the mythic truths buried in her past.

With each book, the world deepens. The shadows stretch longer. And the bond between two souls may be the only thing strong enough to pierce the darkness.

For fans of lyrical prose, slow-burn romance, and the haunting beauty of Celtic mythology, the *Cherry Blossom Series* is an atmospheric escape into a realm where heartbreak births transformation—and love might transcend time.

This series is a collection of novellas. Book four will be released soon.

Other Titles at

beccastormbooks.co.uk

As a self-published author of fantasy, historical fiction, and children's books, I have brought all my titles to one place. With a fantasy series and a historical fiction series published, and two children's books added to my recent book publications, there are several titles to explore. With book one of a new fantasy series just published and more to come in my previous series of books, there will surely be something for everyone.

With decades of teaching experience, I have also created a range of educational books aligned with the Curriculum for Excellence. These books aim to help all learners better understand the skills and strategies necessary for success in the early and first levels of the Scottish Curriculum. However, regardless of your child's curriculum, these skills are transferable worldwide. Although derived from current good practice in Scottish primary schools, these skills form the foundation of all our young learners. Give your child the head start they deserve.

I have also created a range of beautifully designed diaries and notebooks to cater to all your note-taking and personal writing needs. With covers to suit all tastes and lined pages to keep everything neat and organised, no one should be without a notebook to record any inspiration that comes their way.

Children's Books

The Curious Tales of Grim

The Curious Tales of Grim is a magical adventure full of fun, friendship, and just the right amount of trouble—perfect for children who love stories of witches, potions, and talking animals.

With themes of curiosity and consequences, friendship and problem-solving, this series is perfect for 5-7-year-olds when read with a grown-up or for independent reading by children aged 8-12 years.

Daring Donkey

In a world where everyone looks the same and colours are forbidden, one curious little donkey dares to be different. From secret meadows of dazzling hues to the courage to share his discovery with others, Daring Donkey's journey is a heartwarming story about individuality, acceptance, and change.

Perfect for reading aloud or early independent readers, **Daring Donkey** is a lyrical tale that encourages children to celebrate diversity and the beauty of being themselves.

www.ingramcontent.com/pod-product-compliance
Ingram Content Group UK Ltd.
Pitfield, Milton Keynes, MK11 3LW, UK
UKHW020627061125
8801UKWH00032B/358

9 781918 118100